ALSO BY RICK HOWATSON

Guilty Until Proven Innocent

Tales of a
Private Investigator
in Spain

Rick Howatson

True stories of real cases and situations that a
private investigator found himself in.

AuthorHouse™ UK Ltd.
500 Avebury Boulevard
Central Milton Keynes, MK9 2BE
www.authorhouse.co.uk
Phone: 08001974150

First published by AuthorHouse 04/27/2009

ISBN: 978-1-4389-5440-0

Cover design and layout: Alastair Chesson

Printed in the United States of America
Bloomington, Indiana

This book is printed on acid-free paper.

I would like to dedicate this book to Ingrid, my wife,
for being such a good partner and for being there
when I needed her most.

Whether you think you can, or think you can't....
you're right!

Contents

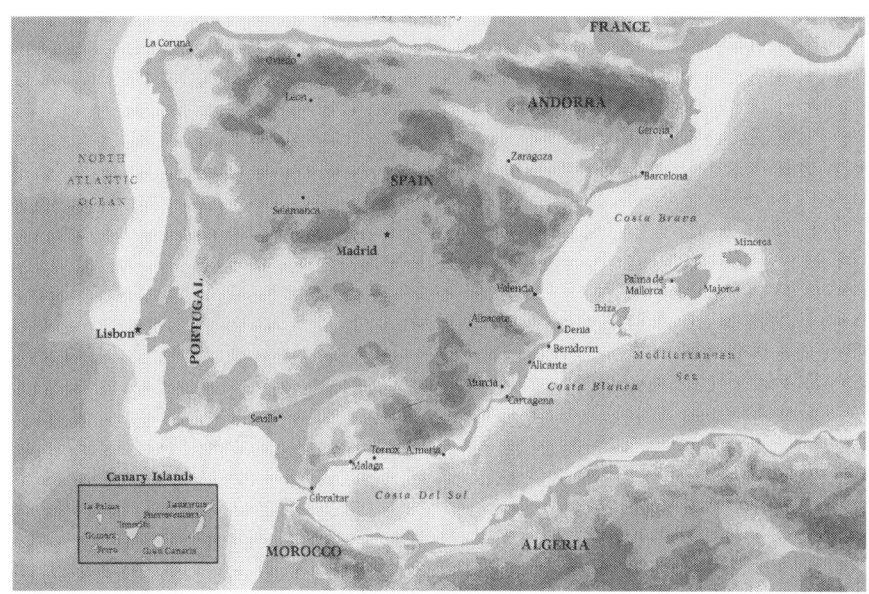

Map of Spain

INTRODUCTION

Why did I become a private investigator? To answer that, you need to know more about me...

At 17 I enlisted in the British Army and became a rifleman, a driver, a scuba-diver and then a diving instructor with Special Forces. My battalion went to Germany, and for four years I travelled Scandinavia, Switzerland, Belgium, France, Holland and the surrounding countries. Leaving the military, I left England, returned to Germany and after studying the German language attended a German medical college in Osnabruck and university for five years. After graduation I worked as an anaesthesiologist for four years before deciding to turn my passion for scuba diving into a profession, and operated a diving school in the Maldives. I circumnavigated the globe, leading scuba diving expeditions in, the Atlantic, Mediterranean, Caribbean, the Red Sea, and the Indian Ocean. I also became adept in several languages.

I would never have believed back then that I would even think about becoming a private investigator.

I met Ian Withers in 1983 in the Seychelle Islands, where I started the first professional scuba diving school there, catering to people from all walks of life; from rock stars to royalty and wealthy tourists who wanted to explore the magic of the surrounding coral reefs and holiday in the island's beauty.

On many an evening Ian would amaze me with the fantastic stories of the days when he was a private investigator in England in the 1970s. Ian was the person who later introduced me to the private investigation industry in the Republic of Ireland.

Ian is not only a worldwide experienced private investigator; he is also Co-Founder and Chairman of the World Association of Private Investigators.

During my time in the Seychelles at my diving school, I trained Jonnie, Ian's 18-year-old son, to become a scuba diving master. Later Jonnie made it his profession and is today chief dive officer and base commander at the South Pole Research Centre.

It all really started some years ago, in the Republic of Ireland, where I had been wrongly arrested and banged up in an Irish jail! When I was eventually released, I discovered that I had been cleaned out by a con man and his wife, big time. So I went looking for them — Jill and Don Pillows, who successfully ran away to hide from me in Spain. This pair cleaned me out of everything that I possessed, and more, during the time I was helplessly locked up in jail.

(If you want to know more, please read my book *Guilty Until Proven Innocent*–Rick Howatson, Trafford Publishing.)

After 16 months of being locked up in a remand jail and 52 court appearances before I was found 'not guilty' on any of the trumped up charges, I was set free to pick up the pieces of my life...

I had however accumulated enough legal knowledge to earn a law degree. It was a pity to let it go to waste; "waste not, want not," as the saying goes.

So I decided to get on with the rest of my life and try to do something with it, try and put a few things right that certain people in positions of power had wrongly done to me. Don and Jill Pillows watch out; THE RAT CATCHER IS AFTER YOU!

I very quickly realised that I had been an investigator all my life, looking for something. Now I believed I had found it: *being* a private investigator.

As a young 50-year-old, out of work and out of home British subject, divorced with no obligations, I thought I would take my new found talent overseas and seek my fortune, and so I decided to take a chance.

Being really serious was not one of my strong points and never has been, but that's what kept me going, and if that's what you need to drive your trolley then that's what you need. Please don't get me wrong, I am not an idiot by any means but life is sad at times, so you have to try and see the funny side of it and believe me it helps. A smile costs nothing.

I didn't have much to smile about back then, but I really appreciated what I had.

I

The Year — 2000
Country of Choice — Spain

To start a business in private investigation here, I realised that I would need some knowledge of the language and Spanish law, together with common sense and thinking logically. So these would be my credentials for this new enterprise in my new chosen country. Unfortunately, I did not know anybody in Spain, nor could I speak a word of Spanish at the time.

The first very important lesson I learnt is that everyone you know is a contact! First I needed to get to know some people, and also renew old acquaintances.

I would need to make some sort of a marketing plan, check out the competition, and see what the overheads of such a business would be to operate. Would there be any profit in it after all the expenses that I would have to pay out?

I carried out market research in Spain with the help of the Yellow Pages; I called some 30 private investigation agencies, or as they like to call themselves, private detectives. To my amazement, not one person that I telephoned spoke English or even my second language, German.

I did some careful record-keeping and listed what salary I could make after taxes, overheads (gas, oil, vehicle maintenance, replacement of tires, replacement of vehicle, telephone/fax, postage, business meals) and a percentage for profit and growth, then I could start to figure out how much I would need to charge for each individual case. At this stage I did not have one customer or even a clue as to what I could charge without being laughed at..

The Spanish are known to be rather laid back, God bless them, and things are very often delayed, put on hold till tomorrow — *manyana*, or to the next day. Clients demand the job be done as quickly as possible, sometimes even before you get the instruction, so *manyana* is out the window for me. I get the job and then get the job done.

One of Europe's big questions in the security industry is whether a private investigator should be licensed and legalised by government to carry out his profession, as is already the case in some European countries.

Spain has one of the most complicated education systems consisting of a five-year university study program. The pre-requisites were laid down by General Franco when he was the infamous dictator in Spain. In other countries, like the UK or Germany, you need only to register as self-employed to become a private investigator.

In Spain as in the rest of Europe all private investigators must be in line with the Data Protection Act that was only just introduced and legislated a couple of years ago here, which unfortunately nobody seems to know much about, or understand.

2

Arriving in Spain

A long ole drive from County Waterford in Southern Ireland, to my new home was about 2000 miles. My cat and I were knackered by the time we got to our new home. My cat Skipper must have thought that we were now New Age travellers (gypsies) with our house on wheels, as we had been travelling in my old VW Golf for the past four weeks.

When I arrived in Spain I was running on empty, like empty pockets; like not much money!

I had just enough money for a small one bedroom apartment and to refuel my twelve-year-old diesel VW Golf and feed my six-year-old cat. I had only £2000 left in my bank account and no possibility of credit. I reckoned that the money I had would see me through for maybe twelve months to start my business and to live, if I was lucky! I had absolutely no other income that I could fall back on, so it really was a case of make or break.

I very quickly moved into the small 1st floor apartment, (that the Spanish very strangely call a bungalow,) but it was fine. I did not see any of the neighbours though; as this was considered low season so no tourists, and no neighbours. I had come to the conclusion that I had moved into a ghost town.

One night a few weeks later, about 2:00 a.m. I heard a noise outside; people talking loudly as if an argument was brewing. I ran to my bedroom window and looked down onto the well lit street that echoed every sound. Below I could see the reason for the noise; to my surprise it was a few old folk walking down the street, very slowly doing the Zombie Walk[1]. (Zombies being bodies that return from the grave — fictional of course!) Seeing this was proof that there is life after death.

I will save you the ordeal of how I got my office set up because it was a very slow process. The Spanish express it well when they say, "Manyana! Manyana!"

My long distance learning courses had arrived from the USA and also from the API, Academy of Professional Investigators in London so I got into reading at every chance I got.

After three months my telephone application was granted and my telephone installed. I then had my Internet connection — the 'umbilical cord' or life line for any business, especially a private investigator.

I named my business *Priority Marine Investigations* and my business door was now open. The only business I had to take care of initially were bills coming in that had to be paid. During the first three months not a single enquiry came in and I was beginning to wonder if I had just made another big mistake in my life!

Locally I was offered a job for the summer washing plates in a restaurant but I politely said, "Thank you," (well I think that's what I said,) "I am not that low on gas yet! But I will keep it in mind."

I had informed just about every person that I knew in the world, about of my new venture in investigation and was really hoping that something or someone needed the assistance of a private investigator, being ME; but things were to start very slowly.

I was offered a job training Spanish policemen to scuba dive for three months. It was interesting, but there was hardly any money to be made in this job. Though the contacts I made here were excellent.

The southern coast of Spain is also the coastal border of North Africa — where the drugs trade is rampant. But first the drug donkeys had to get past the keen eyes of the Guardia Civil[2] coast guard patrols. When the perpetrators knew they had been spotted they would dump their drug cargo overboard. That's where my guys came in — to fish it back out again.

Scuba diving was a life-long hobby of mine and I had been a diving instructor professionally for many years, but now I was getting a bit too old for the job.

But new work was on the horizon!

3

Sunken Boat Wreck — Insurance Claim

I received a telephone call from a marine surveyor that I knew in the UK; he was now a major player in a marine insurance company. A power boat had sunk and the owner was claiming total loss of the motor vessel.

I was really excited. I formed a dive team from the Guardia Civil (Spanish Police)[2] and with the grid reference and details of the unfortunate motor vessel we arrived at the site location and started circular searches in depths of 20 metres.

We dived and covered an area of 500 metres around where the boat should have been, but it was not there. We dived and dived. Ten dives later I came to the conclusion that there was no boat at that location to be found. The under water visibility was very good and it was a sandy bottom so we could not have missed it, and the boat had been reported sunk only three months. What a disappointment for everyone, especially me.

Something had to be very wrong. On this case I had spent a lot of money that I really could not afford, hoping for success. After a week of diving, I reported back to the claims department in the Marine Insurance Company that the boat was not found at the location supplied.

Then it hit me hard. The reality of this profession was: no result, no pay!

I was very depressed to say the least. Now I had to break the news to my dive team; all were so eager and excited and also looking forward to earning some extra money and I just did not know how to break the news to them.

I drove to police headquarters to meet some of the dive team and before I could tell them the bad news one of the guys said, "We need you to check out a boat that we can get really cheap down at the boat yard. We can use the boat for diving." A stay of execution!

I went down to the boat yard that was full of boats being repaired and painted. As I entered the boat yard a motor vessel looked strangely familiar to me although I had never been in this boat yard before; could it be possible that this was our sunken treasure?!

I ran back to my car to collect my camera and as I entered the boat yard again I saw an Englishman with a couple of his mates painting the motor vessel. It is normal to paint the hull, but they were painting just the top sides of the boat. And then the real give-away was when I saw one guy painting over the name of the boat. Mariners would never do this as it will bring you and the boat bad luck. It brought these guys bad luck too, quicker than they could imagine!

I went over to the 'would-be sailors' and asked if their boat was for sale as I was looking for a boat just like the one they were so busy painting, to use as a diving boat.

"Sorry mate we have just bought this beauty," one replied.

"May I take some pictures of your fine boat please"? I asked.

"It will look better in a couple of day's time," he answered, "once we have finished the painting."

I said that I wanted to buy a boat the same size and style as the boat they had. The men had no problem with me taking photos and they even posed by the boat as the new skippers. After I had taken detailed photographs I asked who they bought the boat from and I was told that they bought the boat from an English guy called Tom Madison from Alicante. I thanked the men and took my leave.

This was too good to be true; this was the same boat that we had been diving for. Tom Madison had made the claim for 98,000 Euros. Fortunately, I had photographed the Volvo engine serial numbers on the boat and the name, before it was painted over.

When I called the insurance company and informed them of the find they were very happy with the results. I sent all the evidence and photographs express mail to the insurance claims department in England and I was paid in full for all the work and dives.

The name of the boat was 'SET ME FREE'.

4

My First Case in Spain–
Abducted English Children Taken to France

Cling a ling! My telephone rang! But was this just going to be another wrong number? No; it was to be my very first case. Two children that had been abducted by their disgruntled mother and her new boyfriend, to Toulouse in France. The English courts wanted the children brought back to England and returned to the custodial parent, the father.

I accepted the case and received my instructions per email from the instructing agent in Belfast.

I did not have enough money to drive to Toulouse, so I packed my overnight bag and decided to take the cheaper option of travelling on the long distance coach and walked off to the bus station in town.

The long distance buses in Spain are both good and reasonable, except the inconvenience of the bus driver stopping every two hours and kicking everyone off the bus to wait for him to have his coffee and cigarettes, while we all waited in the freezing cold of the night as the bus doors were locked.

The bus ride was 16 hours and I was really relieved to arrive in Toulouse early the next morning. Toulouse was cold and unfriendly at 6:00 a.m. I had to wait till a breakfast bar opened to get a much needed coffee.

I hired a cheap car at *EuroCar* just opposite the main railway station and drove some 25 miles, visiting some of the villages along the way, and noting the schools in the area. I had been given names of possible villages around the Toulouse suburbs of where the children may be.

Later in the morning I visited the schools that I had noted down previously, as the abducted children were of school age and could possibly be attending a day school in the area. The teachers were helpful but none of them had seen or heard of the kids. As the children were British, they would have been noticed if they were attending a French day school; but no luck so far.

The French countryside looked beautiful with the sun shining. It was really so pleasant and green with wonderful fresh air, compared to the sandy desert region of Cartagena in Spain where I lived. But I had no luck in finding the children and the day was turning into evening. It was now getting dark and too late to carry on with my enquiries.

I drove back into the city of Toulouse but it did not look good. On the streets there were large gangs of 20 youngsters or more, busy with drugs and alcohol sitting in shop doorways, looking as if they had a grudge against society. The most worrying thing was a number of big dogs that the youngsters had with them; it was very intimidating for anyone passing by. The police walked together in pairs on the opposite side of the street, not looking for any confrontation with the youngsters. And I thought New York was bad at night!

I decided it would be safer for me to sleep in my car in one of the little villages around Toulouse so I drove back to a small village, and parked up in a side street and slept in the hire car. The next morning the sun came out and things looked better — apart from my stiff neck.

I got out of the car, cleaned myself up a bit and walked around the village looking for a coffee shop but I found a bakery first and went in to buy some bread.

A sweet old lady was serving behind the counter. I bought a *baguette* [3] and when I paid her she looked at me and said, "Thank you," in English.

I immediately asked her if there were any English people living in the village. She replied that there was a young family with two small children! Was this to be my lucky day?

I asked if she knew where the young family lived and although she did not have an address for them she said she could give me directions to get there. I eagerly made notes of the directions the old lady was giving to me in her amusing Pidgin English and hand gestures.

I thanked the old lady and nearly forgot the bread in my excitement. I followed the directions carefully and after 15 minutes or so arrived at the street where the old lady in the bakery said that I would find the young English family; but it turned out to be an empty barn that had only been inhabited by cows for the last 20 years.

Disappointed, I decided to drive back to the village and find a coffee bar. It was a very picturesque country village alright and as I sat outside the coffee bar on the corner of the street drinking my coffee I was thinking how laid back everything is in the countryside.

After I had finished my coffee I walked around the village again and as I saw the bakery the old lady came out to me and said that I had just missed them! The family had just purchased some croissants a few minutes ago and she had told them that there was an Englishman that had been asking for them. Apparently they said nothing to the old lady in response and left the bakery.

Now I was kicking myself in the backside for missing the opportune moment! I left the bakery and telephoned the instructing agent to give him an update of the current situation. He instructed me to locate the targets and to carry out static surveillance, and if they moved to follow them and not to let them out of my sight. But I had still not found out yet where they were living, so that was a small problem.

It was now midday and the weather was warm and sunny. I drove back to the barns where the cows lived and drove around the area. About 20 minutes later I saw five cars and two of them had yellow English license plates.

I parked the hire car at one end of the street and lay back in the very uncomfortable car seat. There was no movement to be seen from the wooden chalet-type holiday houses, or the cars that were parked outside.

It was now getting on for 4:00 p.m. I decided to go for a walk and get as near as I could to the wooden house to see if anything could possibly tie the cars or the people to the children that I was looking for.

As I walked nearer and nearer to the little house with wooden shutters my heart was just below my throat, beating away so loud I swear I could hear it. Now I was directly in front of the house where the two English registered cars were parked. All the windows had been closed and shuttered, except for one wooden shutter that was just a little bit open on the left side of the house. I ignored everything and walked on down the road and returned to my car.

I waited and waited but nothing happened. But that open shutter was getting to me. Just one little peek could possibly determine and confirm the case. If not, I would have to start all over again. The tension was getting too much for me. It was now 5:00 p.m.

I got out of my car and walked back to the little detached chalet. As there had still been no movement from the house or the street, I casually opened the front gate and walked to the front door. Strangely, there was no doorbell, or letter box with a name on it, anywhere to be seen...

I knocked on the front door with my fist — there was no response. I then walked around to the back of the house and saw the open shutter, hoping to hell that no one had a gun the other side of it thinking that I was a burglar and had come to rob them! I didn't even have an excuse if anybody had put me on the spot and asked me what the fuck I was doing there.

I opened the shutter just a little more and could see a bedroom with children's clothes and toys all over the beds and on the floor. I had a hunch I had come to the right place. After having a good look around the place I was certain that nobody was at home. It was down to some static surveillance now.

I walked back to my car and noticed another house in the street where the lights had just been turned on. I walked to the house and knocked on the door. An old man opened the front door. *"Bonjour monsieur. Commer peut je vous aider?"* Using my 'hands and feet' to communicate, I tried to ask the old gentleman if he knew or had seen the people living nearby. He said that it was an English family on holiday, two kids and mother and father, but he did not know them.

I thanked the old man for his time and returned to my little car. It was now dark and surely the family must return home soon so that the kids could go to bed.

Another lonely cold night sleeping in the car. Nobody came home that night.

10:00 a.m. the next day. There had been nobody coming or going all night and my neck was a stiff as a plank of wood. I was just about to drive back to the village and get some more coffee and bread when my mobile phone rang. I picked up and it was the instructing agent saying that I could now stand down and that I had done a very good job.

I was amazed at what had I done!

Apparently the kidnappers panicked after being told by the old lady in the bakery that there was an Englishman that she thought was a policeman, making enquiries about them. From the bakery they went straight back to the little holiday house, grabbed a few things and left in a taxi for the airport and were arrested trying to board an airplane to leave France.

Job done, I could now return to Spain in that old bus again and go home and get some sleep. First my report had to be written, and more importantly my invoice — one of many, I hoped.

After an uneventful trip back home in the coach and a good night's sleep I went back into my office to see if any work had turned up while I had been away, but it was wishful thinking.

It gave me time to reflect and realise that this profession was a learning game and involved a lot of good luck. I stared at my telephone and then into the monitor of my little laptop computer but nothing was happening.

I now decided that it was time to get a bit more serious about my new life as a PI. I had read the API Academy manuals that they had sent to me for £185 (my long distance learning course) and I began to read them all over again, which made more sense the second time around, while waiting for my next assignment.

Trade associations seemed a very good thing to sign up for, for many reasons. Like networking, making new contacts, assistance from fellow investigators but most importantly, opportunities for work, and seminars to up-date my skills.

WAPI (World Association of Professional Investigators)— based in London, had just been formed, so it was a very good time to join and to paraphrase what a famous man once said, "Ask not what your Trade Association can do for you but ask what you can do for your Trade Association."

As I was based in Spain I said that if I could be of any assistance to the Association that I would be delighted to help. A few months later I was invited to London to attend a meeting of the Governing Council of WAPI, where I was appointed the first Central European Representative for the World Association that I gladly accepted, and I am still the WAPI — Central European Representative today.

I was wondering when the sex, cold coffee and hamburgers would appear — as we see on the TV in *Magnum, P.I.* and it didn't take too long — that is, the cold coffee and the hamburgers; no sex!

5

Pretty 16-Year-Old Russian Girl from Moscow

I received a telephone call asking me if I had time to try and establish the whereabouts of a young 16-year-old Russian girl, who had run away from home and her very wealthy parents in Moscow. I said I would do my best to find her but first I must of course receive instructions in writing, history of the case and a photo of the girl. Once I received this I looked at this pretty young blond girl with blue eyes, wondering what were her reasons for becoming a runaway? Was it school stress, exams too hard or a family member abusing the girl? Or could it be a love affair gone wrong?

Many thousands of young teens go missing every day in Europe and some are never ever found or heard of again, so the parents had a very valid reason to be worried out of their minds because their daughter was missing.

I carried out some ground work but the trail turned cold and the trace ended at Alicante Airport where the girl, Maria, had flown to from Moscow. Maria had not had any arguments with her parents, (or so they said,) and they knew of no apparent reason for their daughter to run away from home. Maria had just left a note saying: 'Do not worry about me, I am OK and I will call you,' but this call never came.

The father found out from a local travel agent in Moscow that Maria had flown to Spain and his daughter could possibly only have had about £200 in her pocket. The police in Moscow had filed a missing person application but could do no more at this time.

Now I depended on the street information, knowing that there is a massive Russian Mafia presence in Spain that run the streets for drugs, prostitution and protection rackets; so if a youngster is running wild on the street they would most likely know about it. I did not want to mess around or get involved with the Russian Mafia though, as it is just too dangerous. No job is worth catching a bullet in the head for.

As this was a Russian job I needed a Russian speaking agent to help me, and I knew just the right young lady for the job. I had met Inga when she first arrived in Spain some months earlier with her parents originally from the Ukraine, but they insisted that they are Russian. When I asked Inga if she could assist me she was immediately excited and wanted to start right away — well after school was out — as she was only 16 years old and attending a Spanish college at the time, so I had to make sure her parents agreed and that they had no objections to Inga helping me.

More often than not, young runaway girls end up on the street or in the legal or illegal, brothels in Spain; young girls from Hungary, Rumania, Ukraine and Poland.

Maria had been missing now for five days and her £200 would be just about finished. If she was not receiving help from someone then she needed help and fast, and if she was receiving help then I needed to find that someone if they existed, and fast.

I drove to Alicante and started visiting the brothels; I was amazed at how many there were mainly on both sides of the main national road. On entering a brothel I casually walked up to the bar and ordered a coke and then looked around to see if I could recognise Maria. Within seconds I had two girls come over to me, asking me to pay for drinks and if I liked them. I said that they looked fine but I was waiting for a special girl; this did create an interest as they said that they were specialists in their trade. I had no reason not to believe them. The girls wanted to know what was so special about the girl I was looking for. This is where things got complicated; if I said that I was a private investigator then a pimp would have me out on the street in seconds, and if they thought I was a cop that could be worse.

At the first couple of brothels I made an absolute idiot of myself, but I had more luck on the street. In the brothels I could not tell the girls what I needed to know, but on the street it was easier as there were not so many ears and eyes around.

When I first spoke to the hookers on the street the first thing they would say was: "Fuck and suck only 50 Euros."

I asked as many girls as possible — 20 or more on the street — about Maria but not many were willing to help me, or they could not speak English or Spanish. I also think they were too scared, or maybe they did not believe me or want to get involved. Some of these girls looked as if they were 14 or 15 years old and I felt sorry for them.

I was surprised to see several black hookers on the street. They started their 12-hour shifts from 4:00 p.m. till 4:00 a.m. The black hookers stayed on their side of the street by the side of one roundabout, The white hookers had claimed the other four roundabouts on their side of the main road leading through the town of Torrevieja.

11:00 p.m. and it was chilly and dark. I saw as many as 30 to 40 girls all in one area on the last roundabout. One older hooker was helpful when I spoke to her; she looked understanding and after a minute or two she opened my car door and got in and said, "Drive." I said, "Hey, wait a minute," but she replied, "You want help? Then drive!" So that's what I did.

She said that she could see by my car that I didn't have much money, so I could have a fuck and a suck for £20. I said that was not what I wanted and she immediately said anything more cost more. I said I could give her £10 for some information, but that was all I could do.

She was curious. "What kind of information you want?" she said and I explained that I was looking for Maria from Russia.

"You a cop?" she asked.

I answered, "No I want to help." She said that she had not heard of any new girls on the street lately but was expecting some new girls the next day from Eastern Europe, but none of them was called Maria as far as she knew.

I showed her Maria's photograph but she did not recognise the girl as being one of hers. This prostitute was from the Ukraine and she gave me a telephone number of a girlfriend that had been there longer than her but only spoke Russian. I said that I would give the lady a call. I gave the hooker 15 Euros and she looked at me and just gave it back. I suppose I looked worse off than she did, but I really appreciated the gesture and I said if ever I could help her I would.

It was very late and cold so I drove to the south of Alicante, a 45-minute drive, to a densely ex-patriot populated part of town where there were many girls on the street and more brothels just off the main motorway. By now I had had enough for one night and went back home to my office to drink some cold coffee.

As I arrived the telephone was ringing. It was the father of Maria. "Have you found her yet?!" he yelled. "Not yet; but we are on the case doing all we can sir!" I answered and added that I would report to him just as soon as I had news for him.

I was thinking about the young girls on the street. It's the oldest profession in the world and it always amazes me how society judges and criticises these young women who sell their bodies, but politicians and business men sell their souls every day and not only get away with it but have no guilty conscience about doing it.

The next afternoon I was now doing the same shift as the prostitutes to try and get some information on where Maria could be. I went to where Inga lived and explained the case to her and that I needed her to make a telephone call in Russian to the telephone number the hooker gave to me. Our ploy was that Inga was the older sister that had come to Spain looking for Maria.

Inga telephoned the number and it was quickly answered by a Russian speaking female. Inga said that she was looking for her sister Maria but the girl on the other end of the telephone could not help us very much and said that with the amount of young girls that arrive in Spain daily from Eastern Europe it was impossible to keep track of them; here today and gone tomorrow. This girl's name was Olga and she said that she would be willing to meet Inga, as she could not speak on the telephone as it was too dangerous. So Inga arranged a meeting at 10:00 p.m. the next evening near the entrance of the Torrevieja Golf Course at a place called Las Ramblers; Inga should be there at 9:55 p.m.

It was dark when Inga and I arrived at Las Ramblers and I could see a security office check-point but there were no guards to be seen inside.

I parked the car at one end of the street and walked with Inga to the meeting point. I was concerned that this could possibly be a trap to catch Inga and get her to work on the streets. One thing you need to learn fast in this job is that you trust no-one. As we waited I disappeared into the dark of the night, just a few metres from Inga so that I could grab her if anything went pear-shaped. After 10 minutes there was no movement and it was damn cold, so I walked back to Inga and said that we should abort the idea and go and get some hot tea.

Just as we walked away from the meeting point a Mercedes sports car convertible came driving down the road at break neck speed straight towards me — this was clearly intentional. I pushed Inga aside and jumped clear myself, into the ditch on the road side. Shocked and scared, we got up and ran to where I had my car parked. As soon as we got there we sprang into the car and locked the doors.

"What the hell was that all about?!" I shouted. Inga was as white a sheet. It appeared that they must have been there a few minutes before we arrived and we had obviously been set up; lucky for us we did not get caught in the trap! But it was a close one and I had a guilty conscience for taking Inga along with me and putting her life in danger; if her parents found out then Inga would never be allowed to go out on a job with me again! So Inga and I agreed not to speak about the incident to anyone.

After speaking with so many street prostitutes and visiting all the brothels in a 25-kilometre radius from Alicante to Torrevieja, there was still no clue as to where young Maria could be. Was she still alive? Or had she been taken to another city in Spain to work the streets?

I was sad and frustrated at not getting a result; we seemed to be so close yet so far away from finding Maria. I returned back to my office after dropping Inga home, to find a message on my fax machine.

```
STOP ALL ACTION. PLEASE STAND DOWN.
Maria has been located in Lisbon, Portugal.
Her father was on his way there to collect
her but he arrived just one hour too late.
His 16-year-old daughter Maria had married a
64-year-old Portuguese man that she had met
in an Internet chat room.
END OF CASE
```

Back in my office I needed work to try and make ends meet and pay the bills. Work was so slow coming in. I sat at my little laptop and surfed the Internet. It was hot outside, about 33 degrees plus, but in my office it was about 40 degrees; no money for an air-con yet. Again I looked at the computer monitor for an email asking for an agent in Spain but there was nothing more going to happen today.

I got my gun out of the drawer and played with it a little. It did look like a real one; but if it was ever be put to the test, I would most certainly be dead! The holster looked really impressive — it was a present from the Spanish police after I had finished scuba diving with them.

6

Two Missing Boys from Dublin

The Spanish autumn was settling in fast and as soon as the sun went down the apartment turned into a fridge. It was cold, I mean really so cold that I needed to get some serious heating in the apartment; but I could not afford it just yet.

Ian called me from Belfast; he needed me to assist an old friend of his in Dublin and when I heard the words 'help an old friend,' I knew it meant was I may or not get paid. I said that I would of course and his friend should call or email me. Paddy, was as his name predicts, an Irish private investigator and his case involved the abduction of two little boys, one three and the other boy five years old. The two boys had been illegally removed from the Republic of Ireland and were last seen two and half years ago in Wales.

The father of the two boys had a court order for his boys to be returned to him in Dublin, as he was the custodial parent.

His current partner, a pretty blond Irish girl called Florence, and mother of the two boys, had fallen in love with a Spanish waiter who had worked in a Dublin fast food restaurant at the time.

To be a waiter was not enough for Jose; oh no, the Spaniard's main occupation was selling hard drugs on the streets of Dublin, destroying families and young lives. Luckily he got caught and arrested by the Irish police and sent forward to the central criminal courts for trial. Jose was held in Mount Joy Prison on remand. After a long trial, Jose was found guilty of drug trafficking and sentenced to 14 years in prison.

Spanish Jose had his sentence appealed with the pretence of mitigating circumstances and was granted a bail application with a £10,000 bail bond tag. Once this was paid he was let out of prison for seven days to prepare his case — or make good his escape.

We know that drug dealers make a lot of money with their evil trade but £10,000 cash was not easy to produce. This bond money had to be in cash, and deposited in the court by an Irish resident who would also be standing guarantee for him. This is where the mother of the two boys came into the story.

Jose had no intention of hanging around in Ireland waiting to be taken back to Mount Joy Prison to serve out his sentence; he had his escape plan already worked out.

Florence, the mother of the two young boys, (then three and five years old), paid the £10,000 pounds bail money and stood guarantee for Jose. The same day that Jose was let out of jail, Florence and Jose took the night ferry from Dunlearghry, across to Hollyhead in Wales with the two little boys.

The story was at one time huge news in the Irish press but soon it was considered old news as no progress had been made in finding the two children; that was two and a half years ago.

Paddy, the Irish investigator, asked me to speak with the father of the two boys so that I could be brought up to speed on the events since the boys had been missing.

That same evening I spoke with Thomas, the father of the two boys, and he was beside himself with worry, as any parent would be under the circumstances. He pleaded with me to take the case on.

I needed written instructions and all the paperwork and any more details that the father of the boys and the agent could give me.

Thomas sent me the newspaper cuttings and the stories of where the boys were last seen and believed to be staying, somewhere in the Welsh countryside, and photos of the two boys with Jose and Florence, and of himself.

The only clue that we had that they may possibly be in Spain was a Spanish mobile telephone number; and the fact that the drug dealer running from an Irish jail sentence was a Spanish national.

No contact had been established in two and half years! Were the boys still alive? Were they in Spain? What did they look like now?

Many questions, and no answers.

Looking at everything we had — and that was not much — our only hope was the Spanish mobile telephone number. So boldly I decided to call the number, using a pretext that I had thought long and hard about. This was a one shot only chance; one mistake and it would all be over. There would be no second chance.

The Telephone Ploy

As my Spanish language was not good enough to speak on the phone, I employed a Spanish professional to make that all important telephone call. I was listening on the intercom as we all held our breath.

A Spanish male answered the telephone in Spanish. "*Dime*" — "Tell me," he said.

"I am very sorry to disturb you sir but we have discovered a problem with your telephone service. No doubt you have noticed that you have been paying too much money for your telephone calls."

"Yes, I have," replied the male voice.

"My name is Juan and I am calling you from the telephone company *Movie Star*. Because your telephone number was cloned by mistake you have been paying two telephone bills."

"I thought as much," the male said.

"Well sir, I can either cancel your number and give you a new telephone number with a credit on it or you if you wish to keep your old number, I can send you the credit that you have overpaid sir!"

"Why can not you just pay the credit to my telephone now?"

"I am sorry sir but we cannot do that as you do not have a contract with us; your telephone is a pay-as-you-go."

"I want to keep my old telephone number," he said.

"That's not a problem sir. If you give me your address where we can send your credit note to, I will arrange for the payment to go out to you first thing in the morning."

"OK," he said, "I am in Benidorm," and he started to tell us his address but just before he said the street name, I heard a distinctive clear Irish female voice screaming at the man.

"What the fuck are you doing, you can't be giving your address to anyone on the phone, you idiot!"

With that the man said, "Send the money to the Subway fast food restaurant in Benidorm; that's where I work and I can get it there."

"That's fine sir. We shall do that and if you have any queries, please do not hesitate to call me. Again my name is Juan from Movie Star Mobile Telephone Company. Have a good day."

I could not believe our luck; Benidorm was just 35 kilometres north of Alicante and a well known tourist seaside town.

Now within five minutes we had found out more than the Irish police, Interpol and other PIs had found out in the last three years. As I have often said, luck is a major factor in this profession.

From my experience just when you want to give up — that's when it all starts to happen! So it's always too soon to give up.

I informed the father in Dublin and Paddy, the Irish agent, of our good fortune. The Father of the two boys instructed me to travel to Benidorm and try and locate the missing boys at once. I happily said that I was on my way.

In my haste I unfortunately did not discuss how I was to be paid for this work. I had given the agent and the father a ballpark figure of what everything would cost, depending on how long I would have to stay in Benidorm and how many other agents I had to employ to work with me. I took it for granted that there would be no problem about payment with the success we were experiencing, but I was to be proved wrong. Just one more valuable lesson that I learnt along the way; when it comes to money trust no one!

I arranged to travel up to Benidorm the same day with a Spanish agent to assist me, explaining to him that we could be away for at least a week or more.

When we arrived in Benidorm I asked the way to the Subway Restaurant, to see if I could identify Jose. I found the subway restaurant easily in the town centre.

We set up a surveillance point to see if we could spot Jose coming in or out of the restaurant. We waited and waited but no sign of Jose, so after three hours I decided to go in and order a burger. There was nobody in the restaurant that in any way looked like Jose! So, disappointed I returned to the surveillance point.

Somehow this was too easy and some thing was wrong! After another three hours I decided to telephone the restaurant and ask what shift Jose was working next.

I called the restaurant. "Who do you want?" a voice asked.

I said, "Jose." "There is no Jose that works here," came the reply.

Shit; had I come all this way for nothing? Then the saving sentence came.

"Maybe he works at the other Subway Restaurant on the other side of town on the beach front."

"Oh there are two subway restaurants?" I said.

"Yes."

"Thanks very much," I said and hung up.

I was relieved and we drove over to the other side of town and soon found the Subway Restaurant on the promenade, beachside.

This time I was too impatient, I had to know at once so I went into the restaurant and bought a burger; and to my delight it was *our* Jose that served me. I spoke in English and he answered with a Dublin accent.

Now that we had that a definite identification confirmed we needed to know where Jose was living and if the two boys were there safe and sound.

We set up a new surveillance point in a parking lot off the beach road and I asked Karl my agent partner to get a cheap hotel for the next few days. I was carrying out the surveillance in the meantime, ready and waiting for Jose to make his move.

The hours past and the Subway Restaurant was clearly closing down for the night and Karl had still not returned with the hotel booking. Karl had worked in Germany in private investigation but not very successfully. But I could not afford to be fussy; I had to take what I could get at such short notice.

Karl was not a bad guy but very money oriented, without much experience and he was not much help at all. I had the feeling he thought he was on a paid holiday, whereas my first interest was to find the missing boys.

The restaurant had now closed up for the night. Unfortunately I did not see Jose leave the place as he exited through the back of the restaurant into an alleyway and disappeared into the night.

Karl arrived and said that he had eaten and that he had also found a hotel for us for the next few nights; as long as I did not mind sharing it with 200 old-age pensioners from Manchester! I aborted the surveillance and went to the hotel and crashed out for the night.

We could sleep in, as Jose was working the late shift and would not start work in the Subway Restaurant until 3:00 p.m. It gave me time to walk around and check out the back alleyway of the restaurant. It was of not much help; there were so many little alleys, one leading into another like a maze, nowhere to set up an observation point to enable us to cover the back door of the restaurant.

So we had to sit it out on the beach front again. We saw Jose in the restaurant but not how he arrived there. This is the point where things start to get frustrating; nerves are on edge and you start saying unkind things to each other.

Karl was getting on my tits, so I left him at the observation point (OP) and started to walk around the ugly high rise buildings that Benidorm is infamous for — they seemed to be everywhere. The residential area was really anti-social, with garbage littered all over the place. Mail boxes damaged, with no names and mostly falling to bits, as they had been broken into. All in all not a very nice place to live and you could clearly see the dealers selling drugs, without fear of the police on the streets.

I was in radio contact with Karl, my partner for the job, at his observation point but he had nothing to report. As I walked down the road a little kid kicked a football over to me. In a friendly gesture

I kicked it back to him and I suppose in his little mind, as a friendly gesture he kicked it back to me!

I was really not interested in playing street football until another little boy came out and said, "Hey Mark who is the fellah?" in an Irish accent. "I don't know," he said, "We are just kicking around."

I kicked the ball back and I called the boys by their first names and they did not question it, just answered yes! Could this be really true that these were the boys we were looking for?

I said, "Hey lads you are really handy with a football; you are bound to be football stars one day. Let me take a photo of you both with the football."

Proudly the two boys posed with one foot on the football and then I wished them well and walked on. I waited around a corner hoping to see where the boys would go next. Bingo; they went into the stairwell and up to the third floor and entered into apartment 32.

I went immediately to an Internet café and mailed the photos to the computer of the boys' father for him to identify his boys. It did not take long and I received a telephone call from a very excited father. "That's my boys!" he repeated several times, "That's my boys!"

Now we had a real breakthrough. The father said that he was on his way over on the next possible flight and could I meet him at Alicante Airport.

I went back to the Subway Restaurant and saw Karl walking up and down the promenade, trying not to be noticed. I informed him of the good news and we closed down the surveillance for the evening and returned to our hotel that was full of old-age pensioners from the UK.

I informed the Irish police that we had a positive identification of Jose and requested an international arrest warrant for Jose to be sent via Interpol to the national police in Benidorm.

The next part of my plan was to keep the apartment block under close surveillance 24/7 until the international arrest warrant had arrived from Dublin, to take Jose off the street and back to jail in Ireland. I informed the national police in Benidorm of the case and that Jose was wanted by the police in Ireland, but to my to surprise the national police were not at all interested. They informed me, "If you try and arrest Jose before any warrant arrives we will arrest you and your men and put you in jail." So much for international friendly relations and European cooperation...

Thomas, the boys' father, telephoned me from Dublin and asked me to meet him at Alicante Airport at 6:00 p.m. the next day. I agreed as apart from the surveillance there was nothing more we could do at that point in time.

Alicante Airport

I waited two hours before Thomas eventually came out of the arrivals hall with two other Irishmen. I recognised Thomas from his pictures in the newspapers and went over to him and introduced myself.

"Hi my name is Rick. You must be Thomas."

"I am," he said, "and I am very grateful to you for finding my two boys."

"Who are these other two men?" I said. "Because I need to speak to you alone."

"The two men, James and Brian, are from an Irish newspaper and are here to report the story," Thomas explained.

"Thomas, they will only get in the way," I said. "Please keep them away, at least until we know where we are and have your boys in safety."

Thomas went over to the two men and said that they should book themselves into the airport hotel for the night and he would call them in the morning.

The newspaper reporters wanted to interview me. I refused and asked them politely to leave us alone as we were not home and dry by a long way yet.

In the meantime is was already 10:00 p.m. I decided that we should also book into the airport hotel as we still had a lot of talking and planning to do.

One of my first questions was: "Do you have the international arrest warrant with you for Jose?"

"No," Thomas said, "but it has been sent from Dublin to Barcelona via Interpol and then to the national police in Benidorm."

But so far nothing had arrived.

I explained the situation to Thomas and that we had to wait for the arrest warrant before we make our next move. Of course Thomas did not agree and wanted to go straight to the apartment in Benidorm and grab his two boys; but I managed to talk him out of it and to follow my plan.

That night I though hard about the situation we were in; I needed two more agents to help with the surveillance. I telephoned Daniel and Robert, two English agents in Denia, and they agreed to come up in the morning to assist me with the surveillance.

All we were waiting for was the international arrest warrant for Jose and as soon as he was out of the way we could go in and the father could get his boys. But it did not work out that way.

Every day I went to the National Police HQ in Benidorm and asked if the arrest warrant had arrived for Jose. The answer was always the same: "No, it has not."

I telephoned the police in Dublin and they confirmed that the warrant had been sent and that Interpol had taken care of it, but nothing had arrived our end.

After a week of continual surveillance and no arrest warrant, one of the newspaper men went to the apartment of the two boys and asked the mother Florence if they could take some photographs of her and the two boys. She told them to fuck off and called Jose.

When I found out what the reporter had done I got really angry with him. I could not believe that this man could be so damn stupid and also that the father was in agreement for him to go there. I ordered Thomas and the reporters to back off and if they did not do exactly as I said from now on I would stop all activities and pull my men out of the job at once and return to Cartagena.

It was too late. On his way home Jose saw Thomas and recognised him; Thomas recognised Jose as well but there was no confrontation.

That night at 4:00 a.m., we saw Jose climb over the balcony of the third floor apartment and run off into the night, and there was nothing we could do about it!

The next morning I was worried that the mother, Florence, would also try and escape with the two boys she was now aware the father of the boys was here and the reporter from the Irish newspaper. The whole situation had to be cooled down somehow before all hell broke out.

I sent Thomas and the reporters back to their hotel as they had been up all night and told them to go on standby; in other words just wait in the hotel until I telephoned them to come. They left reluctantly, but they left.

There was no movement from the apartment and I was also getting impatient now, after two weeks of hanging around. I decided to telephone the number again for Florence. I did not know at that time if she had the same telephone as Jose or not, but lucky again for me she did have the mobile phone.

The telephone was answered. "Hello?"

"Hi Florence, I need to speak with you urgently regarding the boys," I said.

"Who are you? What do you want?" she replied.

"Florence let's not play cat and mouse, I have your apartment surrounded by my officers. The Social Services are waiting to come in and take custody of the two boys; but I would sooner do it peacefully so that the boys do not look back on this day and hate everybody involved," I said.

"So what do you want?" Florence said.

"Meet me in fifteen minutes in the café below the apartment block so we can speak."

Florence agreed and I met her fifteen minutes later as agreed in the cafe, for her guidance and safety. She had an elderly English lady with her, for moral support.

"Now young man," the English lady said, "before we go any further I want to see your identification."

I showed her my private detective badge and ID card, that the old lady studied carefully. She looked at Florence and said, "He is an official, love; you must do what he says."

"What do you want me to do?" Florence said.

"I would like to speak with the two boys for a few minutes and then I will tell you how we go on from there."

Florence stood up and went to the apartment and five minutes later appeared with the two boys. In the meantime the old lady had told me half her life story.

I played a game of pool with the two boys with the mother looking on. I asked the boys how they liked Spain and where would they rather be, in Spain or back in Ireland? They said Spain was OK but they would prefer to be back in Ireland with their mates. After I had lost the pool game to the boys I went back to Florence.

"Florence, I can arrange that you and the boys fly back to Ireland today or tomorrow and that's the best I can do. If you do not agree then I will have to let the Social Services come in and take your boys; so either you cooperate or they have their way."

"What about Jose?" Florence replied.

"It would be better to forget him. You see what happed when he found out we were here looking for you. He ran away like the cowardly dog that he is and left you to fend for yourself. And by the way, he has been arrested and will be taken back to Ireland to serve out his sentence in jail."

I then told Florence that she only had a couple of hours to make her mind up and that she was under surveillance and should she try to escape she would be arrested.

I really left Florence no other options, and I had to be hard for the sake of the two boys.

After she agreed that what I was saying was the only way forward, I asked her to meet with the father of the boys and that I would mediate so that the discussion did not get out of control. She agreed, as long as I was there with her.

I left Florence and the boys plus the old lady in the café and walked over to the observation point and explained to the agents what was going on. I then telephoned Thomas, the father in his hotel but he was apparently drunk and sleeping it off; so I telephoned the reporters to call on Thomas but they were too busy with some hookers that they had picked up.

I sent one of our agents to the hotel to collect Thomas and explain the situation. Two hours later Thomas arrived and we had a very tense meeting with Florence. An hour later the boys were reunited with their father, after nearly three years apart.

That evening I invited the boys, Florence, Thomas and the old lady for a Chinese dinner and the evening went well. The next day the whole family returned to Dublin. The police were waiting in plain clothes and in a friendly fashion took Florence with them for questioning; she was then released from custody.

Job finished successfully? Well no, not quite. Remember Jose the drug dealer? Well the arrest warrant never arrived and the last I heard he is busy selling drugs in Alicante.

When I sent my invoice of 12,000 Euros to the boy's father, I was shocked, as he pleaded poverty and said that the newspaper would pay the bill. The newspaper refused to pay my bill and said the father should pay the bill. So I asked the agent who initially hired me to pay me; he said that he had a legal battle with the newspaper over money as he had not been paid either!

Another lesson learned: Don't trust anyone, and most importantly, do not trust your own emotions as they do not put food in your mouth.

After weeks of wheeling and dealing, I ended up being stung for 12,000 Euros that nobody paid but ME!

7

Infidelity

Times and people have changed over the years but being able to trust your partner has not; it is still the same old problem that it always was. Somebody once said to me that if you suspect your partner of cheating on you, then you are most probably cheating yourself!

One day I received a telephone call from the UK from an agent called Thom.

"I have been given your details by an agent in Belfast; I need an urgent surveillance carried out in Marbella this weekend. Can you do it and how much will you charge me, agent to agent?"

"One moment please I just need to look at my schedule. When do you require the surveillance carried out," I replied.

"From this Friday and for seven days," Thom answered.

"Yes I can fit that in for you Tom. But I will need address photos and instructions received by the morning; can you do that?"

"No problem. And the price?" Thom asked.

This is where Tom put me on the spot as I didn't have a clue what to charge him so I said the first thing that came into my head. "One thousand pounds Sterling, OK?," I said. He agreed at once.

It was only later that I found out that a seven-day week in Marbella on surveillance would cost at least £4,000 but I was learning the hard way and I also forgot to ask for a retainer. But as I said, in this job like everything else, you learn daily.

The next day the instructions arrived by my email and also the photo of a white haired 68-year-old Englishman holding a card in front of his torso stating 'SUSPECT'. The target had been married for over 40 years to his wife, and she was now of the belief that her hubby was having an affair with another woman. The white haired gentleman's name was Mr. Stephen and he certainly looked a nice kind of fellow; but then cheats don't usually have 'Cheat' written on their foreheads, do they?

Mr. Stephen was visiting Marbella for a week's golfing with a group of male golfers and was expected to play on the Naranja Golf Course, one of the better upmarket golf courses for the rich and famous.

I made arrangements for my cat Skipper to be looked after and drove south to Malaga alone. After 600 kilometres I arrived in Marbella. It was my first visit to Marbella and I was quite proud of myself that I found it with out difficulty. In those days I did not have a Tom Tom GPS satellite navigation system. The only system I had to use was 'stop the car, get out and ask'.

I had no money to stay in a hotel or a hostel, as the cheapest hostel was £100 a night; that's Marbella for you. I anticipated this and had a blanket and pillow in the car. I found a friendly petrol station that kindly let me park my old car on their grounds for free.

The petrol station was two minutes walk to the luxury apartments that my subject was staying in. I looked around, made some notes and took a couple of photographs, but my target was not to be seen. I enquired in the apartment reception if the target had arrived and the receptionist kindly confirmed that Mr. Stephen had checked in to the apartments. I was kindly given the telephone number of the apartment that Mr. Stephen was staying in and I left.

In Marbella I was impressed how upmarket everything was and the crowds of tourists that seemed not to have any money problems at all. Lucky devils! I thought.

Now I must be honest, I have never in my life played golf and I would fall asleep just watching it for two minutes on the TV. I have heard it is very relaxing and entertaining, but it is just not for me.

I followed Mr. Stephen for the whole week on the different golf courses around Marbella and it rained every single day. Mr. Stephen stayed in the golf club house for meals and in the evening went for a couple of beers with his golfing pals near to his apartment. No women at all; so I didn't have anything to report.

On the sixth day Mr. Stephen did not play golf but stayed in his apartment. I waited for his next move. I followed a couple in through the security doors and went to the front door of the apartment of Mr. Stephen and took some photos for my report.

I went outside again and waited in the cold and rainy evening. Who would even think of taking an umbrella or a raincoat to Marbella? I didn't even possess an umbrella or rain coat, and I made sure that I left that all in Ireland when I said good bye, along with my wellington boots.

I noticed that two hookers with a poodle went to the security door of the apartment block and pressed the door bell of Mr. Stephen. The security door was released and the hookers went in. I had previously seen the hookers hanging around Puerto Banus area (a very trendy section of Marbella) on the street and in the bars.

Now I had a personal problem with my conscience. My instructions were to find out if Mr. Stephen was having an affair with another woman. Now I can honestly say that I had not seen Mr. Stephen with another woman in all the days he that he was playing golf and drinking with his mates in the evenings; and I could not say for certain that the hookers were actually with him, as I could not see into the apartment.

I knew that if I included the bit about the hookers in my report then his wife would most certainly file for a divorce and I would be the person that blew the whistle and devastated the lives of two people that had been together for 40 years. After an hour, against all odds I decided to telephone the apartment of Mr. Stephen, and acting as the pimp of the two hookers, I asked if the girls were still with him.

A very shocked Mr. Stephen answered, "What girls are you talking about?"

"My girls with the poodle," I said.

"There is nobody here with a poodle," he replied.

"Well just send them back to the bar," I said and put the telephone down.

Two minutes later the two girls appeared on the street with their poodle and walked off into the night.

I wondered if Mr. Stephen would ever have guessed that a soft hearted PI just broke all the rules to save his marriage...

I concluded in my report that Mr. Stephen was clean here in Spain and that he had played golf all week in the rain and that I had not seen him with another woman, which was the truth. Finally I followed Mr. Stephen to Malaga Airport and watched as he disappeared into the departure lounge with thousands of other tourists.

I was very surprised to receive a telephone call from the agent saying that his client was not happy to say the least with my report and that she expected her husband to be caught red-handed.

However Thom the agent said that my cover had been blown and that is why I did not get a positive result and that he would not pay me. My car, a Spanish registered Seat was seen, and that's how the agent knew my cover had been blown.

I said, "Strange; I do not have a Spanish registered Seat; I have an Irish registered VW Golf," and demanded that I should be paid.

I received my money and realised in retrospect that I should have taken a retainer in the first place, but now I knew for the future.

Even if you do not have a *positive* result, it is still a result!

I had a pretty rough week all told with hardly any sleep at all, walking around in the rain on the golf course, so I was delighted that the job had finally finished and I could start on my 600-kilometre return trip, back home to Cartagena.

As I eventually came nearer to home the sun was shining and a new day had begun. All I wanted was sleep for a day or two.

I was so happy to be home again, and my cat was happy to get a decent meal again.

8

Process Serving in Spain

Process service is the bread and butter money for a private investigator and I am always happy to receive instructions to carry out a process service — well, nearly always.

As the months passed I started getting more and more involved in process serving. Being a process server makes you one of the best paid men in the delivery agency business.

But there are three big problems attached to this work:

1. You have to first find the person first that you need to deliver whatever documents that you have to deliver, and give them to the individual personally.

2. In most cases the person that you need to find to personally give the documents to does not want to be found, and as sure as hell does not want to *receive* the documents that you need to hand to him or her, as it could possibly send him or her to jail.

3. In Spain as a direct result of the building boom of the last 20 years there are many streets that have not been given names and many villas, apartments, townhouses and holiday homes that have no house numbers or if they do, there could be as many as three different house numbers, like 327, 67 and 495, all on the same house. So then you have to figure out which is the right one, if any.

So a process service is not a straightforward issue in Spain for a personal delivery of court documents. It's more like a serious game of hide and seek.

There is also one more problem; there are a lot of retired ex-cops and pensioners that are doing the job out of boredom and often serving papers in the area you are working in, for just 50 Euros a time (just an example,) as they have nothing else better to do. I have to compete with this. And they are often unreliable as they have nothing to lose and no taxes or overhead to pay.

Running your own investigation company, it becomes even more important to have a proper business plan at this point. You must be able to determine what special services you can offer to your clients, your professional approach, and your ability to carry out enquiries promptly and professionally etc., to justify the additional pricing well above that offered by a retired pensioner or police officer!

Along with the documents that I receive by special courier service to serve, there is also a letter of instruction. I will be informed if the person to be served is hostile or not; well sometimes, if I am lucky.

I once received documents to be served on a lady in Gibraltar and when I asked my client if the lady could be hostile or not the instructing agents laughed at me saying that I should look at the her date of birth. It stated that the lady was 93 years, old but when I found the lady she was actually 33 years old and she and her husband *were* hostile, because it looked like I was looking for their deceased grandmother. It all ended up to be a big mistake by the Inland Revenue Commissioners' computers — not only was the date of birth incorrect but also the documents.

Can you imagine having to serve documents in a gypsy camp site with maybe ten gypsy families all around you, with angry hungry dogs all over the place and little naked children looking at you as if you have just dropped out of the sky? And you need to serve papers on one of the gypsies, who definitely does *not* want your papers anyway! Then you must officially tell him or her that they have just been served! You are usually miles away from any physical help or civilised society.

I have done this now a few times and each time before I go into the campsite I look for a place where I could be buried afterwards, with the words: "You have been officially served!" on my head stone, on a nice quiet piece of road somewhere, clubbed to death by a baseball bat.

9

Process Service in Torrox

One process service took me to the pretty seaside town of Torrox in Malaga and in the brief that I received from the instructing solicitor I was informed that the recipient of the High Court papers was a very unpleasant man, most of the time drunk and disorderly, and that I should be very careful of him. A nice day out to the sea side I thought, but just in case, Inga came with me on this job so that she could video this guy beating the shit out of me trying to serve him the High Court orders.

We eventually found his little rather rundown ruin of a detached house, on the opposite side of the road from the beach. The front door was immediately off the main road so there was no front garden, only three steps which descended down a stairwell to the front door. I looked to see if Inga had the video camera in place, to film me just about to be killed. I took a deep breath and knocked on the door; an adrenalin rush was looming.

I heard a noise coming from inside the house, someone was moving about. I was hoping that I had not disturbed the man from his lie in or midday sleep, though it was one o'clock in the afternoon.

The front door slowly opened and as I looked down the three steps I saw this rather short, dirty looking miniature Englishman.

"What do you want? he said

"Are you Mr. Andrew Bridge?" I asked

"And what if I am?" he said.

"Well, then I have some thing for you sir."

Mr. Bridge looked at me with surprise. "Who the fuck are you?"

I thought this little man was really pushing his luck; I mean I was nearly twice his size in every direction.

I smiled and said that I was a process server from the High Court of London and handed him the High Court order demanding his presence in the High Courts, two weeks from now.

Mr. Bridge was not a happy bunny as he looked at me and said, "I suppose you like your fucking job, do you?" in a very sarcastic manner.

Again I smiled and said, "Yes it has its good parts," and all the time I was thinking that he was being videoed by Inga. He closed the door in my face and I wished him a nice day too through the letter box. Hey, you win some, you lose some, I thought, but I get paid well for it.

In Spain the process service was a job that was reserved only for the public notaries and the procadura (solicitors) to do at one time. Then came the construction boom in Spain and the public notaries and solicitors became very important and very rich, with their new found work. With the gold rush, little offices turned into prestigious gold mines, so they really had no time to do process serving any more and they really did not care who did it. Now that the building boom is running on empty the public notaries may well be looking for their old job back, but they have made so much money that they will survive well for at least the next ten years.

IO

Repeat Process Serving

Sometimes a private investigator has to re-visit the same person again one, two or even five times with more documents that need to be served upon them and their response is often amusing to say the least.

Mr. and Mrs. Robinson did a very bad job of trying to hide from me on a second visit that I made to their address in Alicante. The first time that I visited them I noticed that the house number had been painted over, but it had been painted over so badly that I could still see the original house number that was supposed to have been covered up.

A lady was standing outside the house talking with a rather obese woman and I saw at once that they were Brits.

"Excuse me," I said, "would you happen to know a Mr. Peter Robinson that lives in this street, house number ten?

"Yes I do," said the thinner of the two ladies. "That is my husband."

"Oh that's good. Could you tell me where he is as I have something for him?"

"I will get him for you," the lady said and with that she entered the gate of the front garden of the house with the painted over house number.

The front door opened and a white male, without much hair and around sixty years of age, came out into the front garden.

"I am Mr. Robinson; what can I do for you?" he said to me.

"Hello Mr. Robinson. I am a process server from the English Courts and I have some documents for you sir."

Mr. Robinson' face froze and he looked as if he had seen a ghost.

"I am not accepting any documents from you," he said in a very disgruntled voice.

"Well sir," I said, "you leave me no other option than to leave the papers here for you." Then I put the papers on the ground in his front garden and wished him a nice day.

I looked back as I saw Mr. Robins and his wife picking up the court documents. I made my report and swore an affidavit with a Spanish notary for the Court in England to confirm personal service of the court orders.

Six weeks later I received another batch of court orders special delivery for personal service on Mr. Robinson, as he had not replied to the first batch of documents that he received from me. After arriving at the address of Mr. and Mrs. Robinson I asked Inga to stay in the car with her camera to take a picture if possible of Mr. Robinson accepting the court orders.

I saw Mrs. Robinson again in her the front garden and I walked over to her and said, "Hello Mrs. Robinson is your husband at home?"

Mrs. Robinson recognised me at once. "Who are you looking for?"

"Mrs. Robinson I am looking for your husband."

"I am not married," she replied.

I said, "Mrs. Robinson please do not give me a hard time; I am only the delivery man."

"My husband is in England," she said, "and will not be back for another month or so."

Just at that moment I noticed a head appearing and then disappearing like a yo-yo at the glass window that was built into the front door. I looked again and recognised Mr. Robinson, jumping up and down trying to get a glimpse of me to see if I had gone or not.

Mr. Robinson reminded me of a little doggie that wants to go out for a walk and is jumping up and down with excitement. I had to smile. Mrs. Robinson now ignored me altogether and walked off around the back of the house. Mr. Robinson was still jumping up and down so I put the court orders into his letter box; it was a tight squeeze but I managed to get them all in.

Mr. Robinson had now stopped jumping up and down and I walked over to my car and drove back to my office. The drive back would have been about 45 minutes and when I arrived back Inga made a cup of tea and we had a good laugh at the behaviour of Mr. and Mrs. Robinson.

I was about to call the notary to ask for an appointment to swear an affidavit of service for the solicitors but before I could pick up my telephone the phone was ringing. It was the instructing solicitors thanking me for a good service of the documents to Mr. Robinson and that it would not be necessary to swear an affidavit as he had already responded to my visit. Apparently Mr. Robinson had telephoned the solicitors and complained about me, that I had put his court documents in his letter box and just walked off! Now if more people were like him and complained more often about how they received their documents, it would save a lot of time and money having to make appointments with the notaries to swear an affidavit. Nice one Mr. Robinson; thanks very much.

I remember one gentleman I had to visit a number of times with documents to serve upon him, in Los Ramblers. The gentleman would invite me in for coffee and apologies for not turning up for court in time and said that he could not find the court room in time.

My instructing lawyers told me another story; that he was so drunk the security officer would not allow him into the court house. But he was a pleasant fellow and made nice coffee.

II

The Case of Tom Hyland,
from County Mayo, Southern Ireland and the
Missing Diggers from China

Back in my office I was checking my messages on my answering machine when I heard the following message:

"Hi there. My name is Tom Hyland from Ireland and I t'ink these bastards have stolen my money and I want you to go and get 'em for me." End of message.

Telephone message number two: "This is Tom Hyland again and I forgot to give you my telephone number, so here it is; six-eight-four-two-five..."

I decided to call the number straight away that Tom Hyland had left on my machine; it was an Irish mobile telephone. To my surprise an answering machine told me: "You have reached the answering machine of Tom Hyland and I am not there."

End of message.

Now I was curious to find out who this Tom Hyland was so I googled him on the Internet, but nothing came up. Late that evening my telephone was ringing again and in a very excited bold and clear Irish accent the voice said, "I am Tom Hyland. Now, can you get the feckers?"

I replied, "Hi Tom, my name is Rick. Get who? Tom please calm down and please explain what has happened."

Tom explained that he had purchased three diggers (known

as JCBs or excavating machines) from an Englishman called Mr. Brown in Spain. The machines were made in and came from China, and the Englishman owned the sole distribution rights of the machines in Gerona in northern Spain. Mr. Brown did not live in Spain; he lived in France.

Now these JCB machines had cost 150,000 Euros and Tom had transferred the money as stipulated and agreed with by Mr. Brown, without even knowing Mr. Green, (an Englishman,) to his bank account in Spain. Tom did not check Mr. Green out at all; he blindly trusted him. However Tom had not received a receipt. Actually Tom had absolutely nothing in his hands to prove that his purchase had ever taken place and that the machines were his property.

At this point it was one man's word against another; who was I to believe? Could I believe that anybody could be that naive and transfer so much money in reply to an advert that he saw on the Internet?

I said to Tom that if he was willing to pay the retainer then I would be willing to look into the matter for him, but I could not promise anything. (In my job there are no guarantees.)

Tom Hyland kept his word and transferred a retainer of 2,000 Euros by Western Union over to me and he also sent me copies of the money transfer that he had made from his Irish bank account to the Spanish bank account for the JCB machines.

I found adverts through the Internet on the website of Mr. Green and all the different machines that he sold. I decided to act as a potential customer, although I had no idea at all at all about these JCB machines. But I needed to learn fast if I was to help Tom Hyland get his money, or the machines, back.

I telephoned and spoke to a young lady who stated that she was the secretary of Mr. Green in Northern Spain. She informed me that her name was Mercedes and advised me that if I wanted a particular machine, Mr. Green could get it for me and could deliver it anywhere in Europe for me. I would of course have to make a money transfer for the full amount before they could consider my order. So now I knew that Tom was telling me the truth; but would Mr. Green keep his end of the deal if I was to place an order with his company?

I certainly did not have 150,000 Euros to find out.

On the upside, I discovered that Tom had received machine serial numbers for the three JCBs when he paid his money. Now I needed to try and establish if the machines matching these numbers actually existed.

I contacted a Spanish colleague of mine, David San Martin in Barcelona and asked him how much he would charge me to visit Mr. Green covertly and try and confirm the existence of the three machines. His price was within my retainer budget so I instructed him to carry out the trace. A week later I received the results with details of where the three JCBs were and confirmation that they really did exist.

They did indeed leave China but had problems entering Southampton in the UK as the VAT (valued added tax) had not been paid and so the JCBs were refused entry into the UK and sent to Barcelona in Spain as this was the location of the dealership, owned by Mr. Green. In Spain two of the machines had been released and were in a warehouse in northern Spain and the third machine was still in the port of Barcelona.

As there had been a dockers' strike, the 35-tonne machine could not be unloaded and was just parked up in the customs pound. The machine was due to be released in the coming days and then to be forwarded to the warehouse with the other two machines, but the problem was that there was money owing that had to be paid before the 35-tonne JCB could be released and then sent by a low-loader by road to the warehouse in Gerona, in northern Spain.

Now the race was on to try and locate and collect the machines — before they were sold on again to someone else.

I needed urgently to meet with Tom, so I called him and reported the progress and that time was now of the essence if we had any chance at all of getting his machines. Tom agreed to get the next possible flight from Dublin to Gerona to meet me.

I traveled upcountry from Cartagena to Gerona by train, which took eight hours and is not exactly an 'Intercity' experience. When I arrived in Gerona I hired a car and checked into a hotel. While I was waiting for Tom to arrive I was thinking of a plan to try and get something in writing to prove ownership of the three machines from Mr. Green. Tom had telephoned Mr. Green many times from Ireland with no success. Mr. Green avoided Tom's telephone calls and was very evasive about answering any questions, said Tom. When asked about the machines Mr. Green just said that he did not know where they were at this time. Already nine months had passed since Tom had paid the full price for them.

My telephone was ringing again. Tom was on the line.

"What the fecken' hell am I going to do?!" Tom said in panic.

"What's the problem Tom?" I said.

"I am fifteen minutes away from Dublin Airport and the plane leaves in ten minutes!

"Tom, don't waste your time talking to me; drive faster!" I said.

Instead Tom stopped his jeep, jumped out and ran the remaining distance to Dublin Airport, as it was faster than driving in the rush hour. If Tom had stayed with the Dublin traffic it would have taken at least another hour and then he would have missed the flight altogether.

Then came silence for the next four hours.

I was really not sure now what was going to happen as I had not heard any more from Tom; whether he got his flight or not. But anticipating that he did catch his flight I made my way to Gerona Airport, to the arrivals hall to meet him. I had no idea what Tom looked like or even how old he was, so it was an adventure to see if he would arrive at all.

I looked at the information monitor in the arrivals hall and saw that the flight from Dublin had arrived on time. I had Tom's name written on a large piece of white cardboard and waited for the passengers to come out and go past me. I waited and waited until the last person left the arrival hall. Maybe Tom had not managed to get on the flight and I could be hanging around doing nothing until the next flight arrived. Or even worse, maybe he would not turn up at all!

I decided to give Tom a call on his mobile telephone and as I did so I noticed a young man just a couple of yards from me take out his mobile telephone.

"This is Tom Hyland."

"Hello Tom, how are you?"

"Jesus, I am fine now. Is that you Rick?"

"Tom, you are wearing a light green leather jacket, yes?"

"I am," said Tom. "How the hell did you know that?!"

"Tom, you are carrying a black leather hold all."

"Jesus — I am. How did you know that?"

"Well Tom, I am a private investigator and I am standing right behind you!"

Tom turned around, and with a big grin on his face said, "Hello, Rick."

I was relieved that Tom had managed to catch his flight in time and not get lost on the way to Gerona. We exchanged "hellos" and drove back to the hotel to talk about the case.

Tom was about 36 years old and a real country lad: naïve, honest and comical.

Tom wanted to go to straight to Mr. Green in the morning and demand that he gives Tom his machines or his money back at once — OR ELSE!

"Or else what Tom?" I said with a smile. Tom, this is not going to happen." I went on to explain to Tom that we did not have a scrap of evidence that he owned the machines or even had any kind of deal with Mr. Green in the first place. We would have to play it by ear; a softly, softly approach; but Tom wanted none of it.

The next morning Tom and I drove the 30 miles from Gerona to Figures, to where Mr. Green was located in a show room on an industrial estate. There was a nice looking Spanish girl named Maria who introduced herself as the secretary of Mr. Green.

We looked around the showroom and Tom got excited when we found one of his machines and the serial number matched his, but there was no sign of Mr. Green. We had no way of taking the machines with us even if we wanted to. I mean, even with the best of British you could not drive a 35-tonne JCB over 2,000 miles along the roads back to Ireland, and then come back for the others.

Maria called us over to the telephone saying Mr. Green wanted to speak with Tom. Tom immediately asked where his machines were and not surprisingly, Mr. Green had some excuses ready.

"Tom the thirty-five tone machine is still in Barcelona in the port and the other two have not been cleared yet. But don't worry you will receive them in Ireland in a few weeks time."

But Tom had heard this so often before. I then talked to Mr. Green as Tom was losing his patience. I spoke using a Dublin accent saying that I was a rather wealthy uncle of Tom's and that I had come over from Ireland to sort out the matter, as I was buying the machines from Tom to help him out. I told him that Tom had borrowed the money for the machines from the family farm account and had created a lot of problems with the family because of this.

I had already prepared a document that I needed Mr. Green to sign, confirming proof of ownership to Tom, but it needed Mr. Green's letterhead on it to be legal.

"Now I just wanted to be sure that Tom had paid for the machines before I would help him out of the shit," I said to Mr. Green.

Now I held out the carrot. "You have a lot of fine looking machines here," I said. "I could do with at least five 35-tonne JCBs for my construction company in England."

Mr. Green took the carrot with both hands and was now as friendly and accommodating as could be. I said that I would see how we go with this deal and sort young Tom out and then I would be interested to place an order for the five 35-tonne JCBs. Mr. Green was so happy he said that he would give me a free Chinese motorcycle just for helping young Tom. I gladly accepted.

I faxed the proof of ownership document to Mr. Green at his residence in France with his own letter heading dictated to his secretary, on his office fax machine, stating proof of ownership of the three machines to Tom and that they were fully paid for.

After several minutes the documents were faxed back to us from Mr. Green signed and in good order.

With the papers now in our pocket I invited the secretary of Mr. Green to come and have lunch with us and she happily accepted.

Over lunch I told Maria about my construction company in England and that I had a holiday home in the South of Spain. I was really laying it on thick. Towards the end of lunch I planted the seed that I may even come over and collect some machines that I would be buying from Mr. Green. Maria said that Mr. Green did not come in the office very often as he did most of his work from his home in France but there was another Englishman that came in every day called Bill and he drove the machines in or out of the showroom, as nobody else could. I paid for lunch and drove Maria back to the show room saying that I had a flight to catch to London that night.

Tom and I returned to the hotel, Tom looked disappointed that we had not got his machines or money back and I explained that we had really done better than we could have ever expected. Now if the case should go to court he could at least prove that they were his machines and that they were fully paid for.

That evening I had a few beers with Tom in the hotel bar; he was a genuine character and full of laughs and I reassured him that everything would work out fine in the end.

The next day I took Tom to the airport in Gerona in plenty of time to get his return flight to Dublin. I returned the hired car to the car rental office that was in the railway station and went into the railway station to wait for my train to go home.

It's always nice to return home after a job it makes me appreciate the small comforts that I have at home that no hotel service can ever provide.

After a well deserved sleep and a few brandies I looked at what we had achieved. I decided to call the port in Barcelona and to make enquiries about the dockers' strike. The dockers' strike is over today, I was told and the JCB that we were waiting for had been taken to a holding yard in Barcelona ready to be collected; but the necessary paper work was needed first and a special rubber stamp of Tom Highland's company in Ireland was needed to stamp all copies of the release documents. I called Tom in Ireland to see if he had this rubber stamp but he didn't and he really did not know what it was or what I needed it for, so I had one made locally.

The next thing was to organise a low-loader and if you do not know what a low-loader is neither did I until that day. It's a very long lorry with an open back, specially designed to carry large heavy machines like three 35-tonne JCBs — and a Chinese motorcycle.

I telephoned Tom and together we arranged for a low-loader to be available at the date and time that we needed it in Gerona.

I arranged to meet the lorry driver in two weeks time in Barcelona on his return trip to the UK. He had a weekly run from England to France, Spain and Portugal and then back again. A rather lonely way to make a living, but the driver was happy with his job and that's what counts.

The driver's name was Mike Dawson and he was from the south of England and spoke with a strong southern English accent. Mike was very nice guy and he was reliable and that was very important; but even more important, he could start and drive the JCBs. Certainly I couldn't; I could just about manage the motorcycle and that was it.

Two weeks later I was back on the train to Barcelona. From the train station I walked to the shipping agents offices where I had to get the clearance documents stamped and signed for the release of the machine that was still in the pound. The stamp I had made for the documents of Hyland Construction in Ireland fitted perfectly onto the documents; the document also confirmed that Mr. Green was to pay the duty for the machine or it would not be released. I was in the handling office for a good hour, desperately hoping that all would be OK, because if it was to go pear-shaped now the expense of the whole plan would be horrendous.

It was now 10.30 a.m. Things went well and I left the handling agents office in the Port with all the release documents signed and ready for the 35-tonne machine to be released to me. As I walked out of the office door I received a telephone call.

"Where are you my friend? This is Mike Dawson and I am in Barcelona but do not know where to go." The timing was excellent.

"Hello Mike. Please drive to the yard in the industrial quarter and look for the holding yard C4 and I will meet you there in thirty minutes," I said.

"Fine; see you there," replied Mike.

I walked around the corner out of the port area and hailed a taxi. "Do you know C4 in the industrial quarter?" I said to the taxi driver "No problem," he said. So I got into the taxi and off we went to meet Mike.

I do believe the taxi driver was taking me the scenic route as the lads in the office had said it was five minutes walking distance, and I had already been in the taxi twenty minutes, but we finally arrived. However there was no sign of Mike and his vehicle. As you cannot hide a low-loader I decided he must be lost somewhere. So I called Mike on his mobile.

"Where are you Mike?"

He answered and said that he was at the security gate entrance, waiting for me. Then I spotted him, in his blue overalls.

"Hey, nice to meet you Mike," I said.

"Same here. I was worried you would not turn up," Mike replied.

"Well let's get this show on the road," I said and off we went.

I went into the offices with all the stamped release papers, only to receive more release papers. Mike had already found the machine parked up in the yard.

I was told that we could have a problem with starting the machine as it had not been driven for some time and also we had to first find the keys. The lads in the office could not help us with the keys and said that they must be on or in the cabin of the machine somewhere. We searched all over the machine; then I remembered Tom saying that he kept them under the engine cover where we looked, and after a few minutes found the keys.

Mike got into the cockpit and started the machine first time; wow. I was impressed. Mike brought this huge yellow JCB to life and after a warming up period he drove it to the back of the low-loader and slowly drove the JCB up on the back of his lorry. The whole thing took about 25 minutes. Now that Mike had tied and anchored down this monster of a JCB we could leave the compound and start on the second leg of our journey — though I really had no idea if it would work or not.

As we passed through the security I handed them the release documents as if I had been doing it all my life, then gave the professional hand wave and we were on our way to Mr. Green's showroom in Figueres.

Figueures is a small town, 150 miles from Barcelona and 35 miles past Gerona city.

Mike was telling me about his life as a lorry driver and how he envied me in my job as a private investigator. I explained that Tom had been caught up in a possible scam and I was doing my level best to get him out of it.

The roads were not too busy so we made good progress and arrived in Figueures about 3:00 in the afternoon. As we pulled up outside the showroom of Mr. Green it looked all closed up. We were now in the holy hours of Siesta in Spain. From 1:30 p.m. to 4:30 p.m. is rest time. This is the hottest time of the day and people do not want to be disturbed. Many people go home to sleep; most of the shops close and people take their afternoon break. But in fairness to the Spanish, they come back and work till 8:00 or 9:00 p.m. in the evening.

I climbed out of the cab of the low-loader and walked over to the showroom door and I could see Maria eating her sandwiches. I waved to her and when she waved back. I beckoned her to come to the door. I could see that she was not too happy about doing this but she did come over and opened the door to me.

"Hello Mr. Hyland, I did not expect to see you today."

"I had informed Mr. Green that I would be coming but was not sure of the dates because of the low-loader's schedule."

"I am sorry," Maria said, "but Mr. Green is not here today."

"Ah no problem. We can manage without him," I answered.

Then I showed her the paper that she herself had typed and Mr. Green had signed, confirming that the two machines and a motorcycle were paid for. She said that she needed to telephone Mr. Green. I said, "Please do; but do not take to long as we have to get to the ferry boat on time to make the reserved crossing from France to Ireland."

Mr. Green was not to be found and in the meantime Mike had come in and started the machines for the warm-up. I opened the huge show room doors and Mike drove one of the machines over ready to drive up on his low-loader, Maria came running towards me.

"What are you doing?"

"We are collecting our machines, as we said we would."

"Please come to the office. I need your passport at least and you must sign for them," Maria said.

I walked back into the office and Maria took my passport and made a photocopy of it. Maria did not even notice that it had a different name than that of Highland. Maria then produced an invoice for me to sign.

In the meantime Mike was busy driving the two machines onto his low-loader. I signed the invoice for Maria and asked her for the paperwork of the machines and the motorcycle. Maria went into the back room of her office and at the same time I picked my passport up and the photocopy that she had left in her photocopy machine.

Tension was building and the adrenaline pumping because I was the only one that knew what was really happening and I was making it up as we went along! Maria returned and said that the papers must be in the machines as she could not find them in the back office or Mr. Green would have them. Lucky for us Mike had found the papers under the seat in the cabin of the JCB. Maria said that she would telephone Mr. Green again or Bill his partner to come at once, as she could not accept the responsibility of releasing the machines.

"Maria please do not worry my dear I will accept the responsibility. Mr. Green is aware of everything," I assured her.

But Maria was no longer listening to me she was too busy trying her best to get Mr. Green or his partner Bill on the telephone.

I looked outside the showroom and saw that Mike had the machines loaded, and the motorcycle that was still in a huge carton box was just being put on with a fork lift that Mike found in the warehouse. Mike was the star of the day and it was brilliant that he could drive all the machines. Otherwise I would have been well and truly up the creek without a paddle...

I looked back at Maria busy on the telephone and walked out towards Mike.

"Everything is loaded now and I will only need ten minutes to secure all the straps down," Mike said to me.

"Mike you do not even have ten seconds; we are leaving right now." Mike was excited. "Sure thing," he said and jumped into the cab leaving the fork lift on the side of the street. I climbed into the cab and off we went.

Mike said that this was the most exciting job he had ever done and was thrilled. So was I — we had managed the impossible — but it was not over yet. We drove five miles down the road and then pulled over in a lorry park to secure the machines and the Chinese motorcycle. I stood on the side of the road expecting Mr. Green or his partner to be on our heels with a lot of heavies, but it did not happen so we carried on in the direction of France.

I left Mike at the Spanish-French border town of Perpignan and I watched as Mike drove his fully loaded low-loader over the Spanish border into France.

I got a bus ride back to Figeures and then made my way to the train station and got a train back to Gerona with a connection back to Cartagena. Twelve hours later I was back at home reporting to Tom Hyland that his diggers were on the way to him in Ireland. Tim was delighted, as well he should have been and I was delighted that everything went well.

I had really enjoyed playing the rich uncle from Ireland, Mike was happy and he sent me an email asking if ever I needed help again he would love to be in on it — so I suppose the only person who was not happy was Mr. Green and his partner Bill.

Strange ole life...

END OF CASE

Back in the office my old cat was happy to see me; it was nice having this loyal little friend for life waiting for me when I returned home. I named my cat Skipper; he was born in my bedroom when I was still living in Ireland. He was the ugliest cat of all the litter and nobody wanted him; but from this ugly duckling grew a very large lovable, tabby tomcat and he was a part of the family. Whenever I had to go away for a few days Skipper, my trusty cat, would be looked after by one of the old ladies in my street. But it was as if he had a built in radar system or tracking device on me, because he always knew when I was coming home and would be there waiting for me at the front door.

12

Did Hendron Come Back to Even the Score?

Another true story

I am still a private investigator working in Spain on the 'Costa del Crime' and a couple of months ago I received a telephone call at midnight from a neighbour asking me to take a look at an old Belgian gentleman who lived on the same street as myself. He was terminally ill with cancer and in great pain, but refused to go into hospital.

I telephoned the old man at his home saying that if he needed any help that he could call me; and one hour later that night he did!

This 79-year-old gentleman's name was Hendron. He lived all alone in a little semi-detached house known as a *quarto*. His wife had passed away three years earlier, also a cancer victim.

At 1:00 a.m. that night I went to Hendrick's home and found the poor man in agony. I said that the only way that I could help him was to take him into the local hospital Los Arcos, about 7 miles away. Reluctantly he agreed and I carefully lifted this frail man of about 85 pounds and put him in his car and drove off to the local hospital.

It was a long night; the doctors thought that I was Hendrick's son; age-wise that could have been possible. The doctors informed me that they did not expect poor Hendron to live much longer than a day at the most. I stayed the night at Hendron' bedside, thinking how sad it was, such a final goodbye. Hendron told me his story:

Six years before this sad night Hendron, his wife and the wife's brother Robert with his wife, made a decision to move to Spain. They were all Belgian nationals and all wanted to accept the challenge of a new life in the sunshine and live in Spain. Now that they were all pensioners what worries could they possibly have? Their pensions were paid in regularly into the bank and they could manage well on the Spanish economy.

Robert and his wife lived next door to Hendron in the other half of the semi-detached quarto and at first everything was grand. But then Hendron' wife became very ill and Robert blamed Hendron and said that it was his fault that his sister was so ill. The relationship deteriorated so badly that Robert sold his little house and moved to another part of the village. He did not move far, but far enough that he could not see Hendron, and the family lost all contact, refusing ever to speak to Hendron ever again.

When Hendron' wife passed away, Robert, instead of supporting his brother-in-law in his grief, blamed him for his sister's death. With the loss of his wife and the cruel unfounded accusations of his twenty-year-old younger brother-in-law, Hendron fell into a deep manic depression. Hendron had been happily married for over fifty years.

I left Los Arcos hospital at 6:00 in the morning, really tired. The doctors said that it was nearly over for Mr. Hendron as he now had kidney failure. When I got home I had a coffee and then decided to telephone Robert the brother-in-law and inform him of what was happening. I did not want to get involved in this family feud but at the same time maybe Robert, a devout Catholic, would surely show some compassion and understanding, now that his brother-in-law was dying I thought.

I do understand that 7:00 a.m. is an ungodly time to be telephoning anybody but I thought that the urgency of this matter warranted it.

I spoke in English to Robert, who said he was aware that his brother-in-law was terminally ill, but it really did not interest him and that he had not spoken to the man in over three years and that he was responsible for the death of his sister. I explained that this was not the time or place to be making such terrible statements; I was after all just a neighbour running a humanitarian errand. I explained that the next of kin should be informed and that if anyone would like to see him that he was in the local hospital.

I still had the keys to Hendron' car and home and Robert asked me for them. I said that I was sorry but I could not give him the keys but he could collect them from the local police station later that day.

Now that I thought that I had done more than my neighbourly duties, I went to bed and crashed out.

I woke up about 3:00 in the afternoon. I was wondering if the old man had passed on or if he was still suffering. You know things like that stay in the back of your mind for days, and the whole question of the cycle of life and death hits you again.

I got out of bed and made my way to the outside shower. It was another beautiful day of pure sunshine, without a cloud in sight. I drove into town to do my shopping, picked up my washing and spent a few hours in a new computer shop that had just opened up for business; the first computer shop in our town.

I arrived home, showered again and freshened up and gave the hospital a call to see what time the old gentleman had passed on but I was surprised to hear that he had not passed on at all but had, in fact, been picked up by Robert and taken home. Now this I just could not understand at all. I got dressed and was annoyed that I was now so involved in this sad story and to my surprise my telephone was ringing and it was Robert on the other end.

"What shall I do?" Robert said, "He is dead!"

I took a deep breath. "Robert where are you?"

"I am at Hendron' house."

"Are you alone?" I said

"Well I am now. Yes. What shall I do?" Robert said again.

"How do you know he is dead?" I asked.

"He is stiff as a plank of wood," Robert replied.

"Have you reported the death to the police yet?"

"No I haven't."

"Robert, call the police at once explain to them where you are and what you believe has happened and I will come over once the police have been to the house."

I walked to Hendron' house and I saw Robert standing outside and I asked him what was going on. Robert repeated himself, saying that Hendron was dead. He said that Hendron wanted to die in his own home, so he brought him back to his house from the hospital to let him die there as per his wishes.

Again Robert asked me for the keys to the house as he only had the front door key that he found that was hidden under a flower pot.

"I did not have them anymore as I have already handed them into the local police station in the village," I told him, and asked if the police had been called.

"Yes they are on their way," was the reply.

Nothing much really happens in our street but today was to be a field day for the local gossip. The neighbours were all busy exchanging ideas about what could have happened here and the whole street knew that Robert and Hendron hated each other. So it did not look too good for Robert; and when the police car arrived that really did add colour to the proceedings.

The police called a hearse to collect the body after the local doctor had certified the death of Hendron; the corpse was then transported away for a post mortem and a sombre shadow fell over the house.

I went back to my office and did what I do best — write a couple of invoices and check my computer. Work was still slow coming in and so I had no stress and had plenty of time to think about the past sad events.

Two days later I was biking down my street when to my absolute horror I saw about eight people all in the house of Hendron. I stopped and looked inside. The people were going through all the old man's belongings; and I mean *everything*, like vultures after the kill.

Robert, the brother-in-law of Hendron, spear-headed the crowd of neighbours. Robert saw me and beckoned to me to come into Hendron house; I went to see what he wanted from me.

"Hey, come here Rick! This jacket will fit you and you can have it, my friend."

"No thank you, I would not be interested in anything of Hendron' clothes or belongings."

Robert then said, "At last I'm getting something from my brother-in-law."

He wanted me to see the spoils of the day but I really was not interested, just disgusted, and excused myself and walked out. All around the house people had all the cupboard doors and drawers open and were busy sifting through all that they could find with the excuse that the place was dirty and needed cleaning up. Cleaning up for who, I wondered? More like cleaning out!

I know that when I clean up at my home I am always finding things that I did not know that I had anymore; maybe Hendron forgot that he still had these things, or maybe not! Hendron was a collector of everything and among his collections he had two 9 mm handguns and a rifle and lots of ammunition hidden away in his house. I did not know about this till later.

It's always like a race here in Spain when you throw things away. You take something to the garbage bins (or wheelie bins as they are known here,) like a shirt or an old pair of jeans, and hey presto they're gone in minutes. There are plenty of poor people that delight in the things that the better off throw away. It's nice to know that the things will be used again; "waste not, want not" is the motto here in Spanish 'bin-land'.

A few days later Robert called me to show me something that he had wanted for a long time he said from his deceased brother-in-law; the two 9mm handguns, ammunition and a rifle. I suggested that he should hand the weapons in to the police at once. Maybe a crime had been committed with these weapons or somebody could break into his home and steal them and then go out and kill someone else. But Robert had absolutely no intention of handing these illegal weapons into the Spanish police or any other police. Then he asked me if he could work with me as a private detective so that he could get a license to keep his newly found toys.

"No way Jose, private investigators do not use guns, they use their brains," I told him.

Then I did my best to explain the implications of his stubbornness and how dangerous it was to have these weapons; they are not toys and with the terrorist situation as it is he could go to jail. But Robert said he would keep the weapons, so that if he ever had his house broken into he would shoot the perpetrators; he had no intention of handing his weapons into the police.

I told him that some people never cease to amaze me; that he was a 60-year-old man and should really be more mature and responsible. Again I advised him to hand them in to the police as they did not belong to him; they were still the property of Hendron.

As I left Robert's home I could see that he was happy playing with the guns in his front room. I was just thinking how incredibly ignorant of the man to have the cheek to ask me to put my hand on his head to pronounce him a private detective (as if I could,) just so that he could keep his illegally gotten guns, that he stole from his deceased brother-in-law.

Weeks went past. Hendron was cremated and his urn and ashes were put in the undignified bicycle shed by the side of his house and I was told that he would never be allowed into his house again.

As a private investigator I do not know to this day who informed the police or how they found out about the weapons and who alerted the anti-terrorist swat team that visited Roberts's house in the early hours. I was away on a job when I heard that the Spanish SWAT team and officers from the anti-terrorist unit with three police cars raided Roberts's house and took him away in handcuffs. News travels really fast in our little village…

Robert was later charged with illegal possession of fire arms and is on a waiting list to appear in the criminal court after handing his passport into the police so that he can not leave Spain.

Two months later, I received a visit at my house from Robert; he was very excited, angry and shouting at me.

"It could only have been you that reported me to the police!"

"Robert, what on earth are you talking about?" I said.

Robert went on to say that he had just been released from the police station and that he had been arrested and his house was searched, his handguns and rifle had been taken away from him and he had been charged with being in possession of illegal weapons and could go to prison or be deported. Now he was under house arrest with his passport confiscated by the police.

"Robert, I do not know what the hell you are talking about, I have only just returned home from an overseas assignment," I replied.

As Robert stormed off he had made so much noise that the neighbours came to see what all the fuss was all about.

One of the neighbours shouted at Robert.

"You mean bastard, how could you have treated poor Mr. Hendron so badly. We are glad that the police have come for you. Everyone in the street knows about all the things you have taken from the poor old man's house."

Robert shouted back at him, "So it was you who told the police, you bastards!"

The neighbour replied, "No; but I wish it had been."

The mystery is — who DID tell the police?

As a private investigator I do not know to this day who informed the police or how they found out about the weapons, or who arranged for the anti-terrorist swat team to visit Roberts's house in the early hours.

So who did inform the police about the illegal guns in Roberts's house? What goes around comes around in this life...

Did Mr. Hendron perhaps have it planned, knowing that Robert would not resist the temptation of taking his guns? Or did he tell the cops from his grave? We may never know...

END OF CASE

13

Tracing Missing Persons

There are many reasons why a person may need to be traced or why they go missing in the first place, so it is imperative to know who is instructing you and why the person is to be traced. There have been cases worldwide and especially in the USA, where people have been traced by a PI, who has then been murdered, or stalked by the person who instructed you to trace the person.

Skip traces are carried out when someone owes money and has done a runner to avoid payment, so the enquiries must be carried our discreetly because otherwise the subject will just move on again.

I had received instructions from a solicitor in England that he needed me to trace a man and his family, for family reasons. The solicitor was well known to me so I had no problem with carrying out his instructions.

The area I had to visit was in Almeria, about 150 miles from my office and I had the chance to use a friend's car as my car was being repaired. My friend, a television repair man, had a broken leg so he was off work. I gave him 50 Euros for the hire of his van. It was the perfect under-cover vehicle.

Once I arrived in Almeria I had another 60 miles to drive inland towards and into the rocky mountains and desert. After 40 miles the roads turned into just dust tracks and from here on it would have been better to have a camel.

I stopped at a small outpost of the Guardia Civil and asked the duty officer if he knew of the subject that I was looking for; he did. The officer told me that the Englishman had a car accident six months earlier, but it was only damage to the car and truck nobody was hurt. He explained that the man, being the only Englishman in the whole area, lived in a very small village 20 miles further on into the mountains. My old VW Golf would not have survived this trip, so I was happy to use my friend's van.

After a few miles the road got better and in the distance I could see a village. Once in the village I found the small shelter of a house that the subject lived in with his wife and three children. I went to the neighbour's house to make discreet enquiries, but before I got to the front door an old Spanish gentleman came out of his house and said that he was waiting for me!

I asked the old man if an English family lived next door to him and he answered, "Yes they do but they are not in at the moment. Come in and fix my television." I replied that I had not received a service call to go to his house and that I was looking for the English family.

"Don't be concerned about them. Come and fix my television," he repeated.

At the point I have to admit that I am a man of many talents, but fixing televisions is not one of them.

"I am sorry but I can only look at it when I receive a service call," I said hoping that would satisfy the old man; but no such luck.

"Come; I will give you five Euros extra if you fix it for me," he said.

I had no other choice so I went into the old man's house and looked at his TV, but I really had no idea at all what the matter was. I wrote down the model of the TV in my notebook and switched the TV on but it was as dead as a doornail. I gave the TV a knock and then again; and would you believe, the thing started. I smiled at my luck and said that it was just a loose connection.

The old man was happy and asked, "How much do I owe you?" "That's OK sir no problem, no charge. But tell me, when do you think the English family will be returning home?" I said.

The old man answered, "They are on their way back now; I can see the black jeep coming over the mountain."

This was time for me to get the hell out of here as I did not want them to see me.

"I will be off now," I said to the old man.

"Here take the money," he insisted.

"No, this is a freebie," I said, "but if I have to come back again then I would have to charge you."

The old man smiled. "You are an honest man," he said to me. "Thank you sir."

I quickly left his house in the TV repair van and drove off, just in time to see the Englishman and his family passing me and stopping outside the house next door to the old man's house. I could see that the old man came out to speak with the Englishman as I turned the corner and off down the track homeward bound. That was a tight situation! If my cover ever gets blown on a job then the job is immediately aborted. Which also means no money!

When I arrived back at my office I wrote my report, but before sending it I decided to call the solicitors to give them an update and also to ask what the hell had this poor Englishman done to deserve such a punishment to live where he was. I would have preferred jail than to live in that god forsaken hole in the desert.

The solicitors said that the Englishman had done nothing wrong at all. He had an argument with his mother and run away without telling her where he was going to and that was over two years ago. The mother knew he had gone to Spain, but did not know where! I said to inform the mother that it was not a place to go for holidays and the coast was at least 100 miles away.

Well at least the old man got his TV fixed; or did he?

END OF CASE

14

Asset Tracing

Back in the office in Cartagena things were looking up, work was coming in and like any business one day I was up and the next I could be down again. That's the risk you take in any business when you are self-employed. You have to sell yourself and sell yourself well while you can. Or as Captain Jack Sparrow from 'The Pirates of the Caribbean' would say, "Take it all and give nothing back." Well, something like that.

Mondon is a very typical romantic little Spanish village in the south of Spain with tiny narrow alleyways called streets, where hardly a car could drive between all the buildings, which without exception were all painted white.

I was sent there to try and trace assets in a nasty divorce case that was currently going on in the High Courts in England. The couple divorcing had been married for 25 years and for the most of the 25 years the man Mr. Branson had been living off his successful wife's self-made business without any contributions of his own.

Mr. Branson had been partially unemployed, and had lived in Spain off and on in a small family holiday apartment in Malaga and had nothing to do with the day-to-day running of his wife's business, except helping himself to money whenever he could.

Mrs. Branson had accumulated three children's nurseries and employed 50 staff to take care of the small children that their parents would entrust to the nurseries early in the morning til the afternoon, so that the parents could go to work to pay the fees for the care of their little ones. This was a very lucrative business.

Mrs. Branson believed that Mr. Branson had been siphoning money from the family business accounts; but in the divorce courts Mr. Branson declared with a tear in his eye to the court that he was penniless and had absolutely nothing, and therefore his beloved wife should pay him a whole load of money in a settlement!

I was myself quite surprised on checking the Land and Property Registry that Mr. Branson actually owned *four* townhouses, one being a penthouse. On checking the company registration I found that Mr. Branson had a bar and also an estate agency in Mondon. When I informed Mrs. Branson's solicitors of my findings they were delighted and asked me to take photos of the properties and get up-to-date evaluations of all the assets.

As I mentioned, Mondon is a very small village in the south of Spain near Malaga and was not hard to find; but once I had arrived I had to leave my car outside the village as the streets were too small to drive a car through, creating one of Spain's first 'pedestrian only' zones.

It was a piping hot day, about 33 Celsius plus, and not really an ideal day for walking around in the heat, but it goes with the job. Once in the village, (that housed some 2000 inhabitants,) I walked the narrow streets to try and find the addresses of the properties that I had located for Mr. Branson, and that was not easy.

The first few people I asked had not heard of the street names and there was no police station or tourist information office that I could enquire at.

After an hour of walking in the heat I found a bar and bought a large bottle of water and asked people in the bar if they knew of the street that I was looking for. This time I had to be careful because there were English people in the bar and I did not know what Mr. Branson looked like. I did not even have a description of him and I would not like the embarrassment of bumping into him by mistake and asking him where he was hiding his assets.

Luckily for me (and remember what I said in this job, you

certainly need luck) the street that I was looking for was just around the corner from the bar, so off I went.

As I arrived outside the town house I could see a big notice: "SVENDE" — this being a 'for sale' sign — hanging from a top window. As I took a couple of photographs the front door opened in front of me and three people came out of the house, two men and a woman and they all looked very pleased with themselves.

I quickly realised from what I could hear that this was an estate agent and that the couple had just purchased the property. I approached the group and said that I had come to enquire about the house that is for sale. The estate agent proudly said that he had just sold the house to this wonderful couple. I expressed my dismay saying that I had seen that the house was for sale with my wife a week ago and was now coming to make an appointment to view the property.

The estate agent took me to one side and said, "Look there are more properties for sale from the same owner; he owns a bar not far from here. If you go and see him I am sure you will get a fantastic deal as he needs to shift (sell) all his properties as quick as he can, as he is in the middle of a divorce case and his wife was trying to fleece him."

Out of interest I said, "How much did this house sell for?

"A hundred seventy-five thousand Euros, plus seventy-five thousand Euros black money," the estate agent informed me.

'Black money' is undeclared money paid in cash at the time of closing the sale of the property to avoid paying sales tax, so it is a benefit to the buyer and the seller, but not to the Spanish finance department. The Spanish government has looked into the black money issue and it is now officially illegal and only done with a big risk today in Spain and, if anyone is caught, heavy fines are imposed.

The estate agent said, "When you go to the bar do not forget to say that Jerry sent you, and ask for Mr. B."

"I won't forget," I promised and thanked him very much.

The bar was only five minutes walk from the townhouse that

had just been sold in the centre of the village. There were only two bars! Not much entertainment in the long summer evenings.

A very old English gentleman with a white beard propping himself up behind the counter of the bar, who looked about 80, asked me what I would like to have. I came straight to the point and asked if Mr. Branson was there? "He is," the old man said. "He is upstairs in his apartment but he will be down in a few minutes."

I ordered a Coca Cola Light and sat down. It was a dirty rundown bar and certainly not the sort of place you would like to take your young lady for an evening out. A few minutes passed and I saw the old man from behind the bar pointing across at me, talking to a red haired gentleman, who I now know is Mr. Branson.

I took an instant dislike to Mr. B, as he came over to me and said,

"Who are you and what do you want?"

"Jerry sent me," I replied, "as I am interested in buying a property for me and my wife."

"How much do you want to spend?" he snapped back at me!

I did not like Mr. Branson's blunt attitude at all but I was acting humble pie. "Well," I said, "that depends on what you have to offer?"

Then to my surprise and delight wonderful Mr. B produced a paper with four other properties for sale with the actual price *and* the black money required for purchasing the property.

Mr. B said, "The properties are only for quick decision makers; they are real bargains and have only just been made available and will not be on the market long. This bar is also for sale, along with three-bedroom living accommodation above the bar."

Mr. B went on to say, "The business potential is huge because of the location in the middle of this beautiful Spanish village, and if I was not moving to Australia I would stay. That's the only reason I am selling up as I have been living in Spain for ten years and love it."

I thanked Mr. B, asking when it would be convenient to visit the other properties. "You have met Jerry, call him and he will show you around tomorrow as he works for me," he replied.

I really did not expect to have so much luck in one day.

I discovered that Mr. B had been buying run-down properties and cleaning them up and selling them on with a handsome profit. And as he owned the estate agency and all the properties he could fiddle the books as he liked.

I walked around the village, taking photographs, as I now had a legitimate reason for doing so; the bar, the estate agency and the properties.

When I was finished it was late and by the time I had found my car again it was dark and time to be driving home; I had really done enough walking for one day. It took me six hours to drive back to Cartagena from Malaga. When I arrived home I sat in front of my computer writing my report and down loading the pictures, plus scanning all the title deeds I had collected from the Land and Property Registry and emailing them over to my client.

After I had finished the reports it was already getting light again and so I crashed out for a few hours on my sofa, with my faithful cat Skipper by my side.

I woke up as the telephone was ringing and when I answered I recognised my client's voice. "Well done, very well done. You have done a really fantastic job."

"Thank you," I said.

"Now we will need you in court in three week's time, to be a witness!"

My first case in court; I needed to prepare myself well so that there were no hiccups. I made sure I had all my paperwork and original reports and photographs and to be sure, I called an old friend of mine in Belfast just to get his expert advice. So I was now fully prepared.

The three weeks passed quickly and I was ready to go. Inga gave me a lift to Murcia airport. My flight was delayed seven hours, then I had to fly out from Alicante Airport instead of Murcia Airport due to fog. Thus I arrived nine hours late to meet my client, who had patiently waited for me at Gatwick Airport arrival hall, all night.

I was taken to a nice hotel and told that the solicitors wanted to speak with me before court first thing in the morning. I was hoping they would. I was collected from my hotel and taken to the solicitor's office where again they said what a brilliant job I had done as Mr. B's wife was not aware of what her ex had accumulated over the years and where all the money had gone. Now she had evidence that she needed to prove that it was over a million pounds. After speaking with the solicitors I was introduced to Mrs. B and she seemed like a very nice lady and somehow far to good for the arrogant old fart that I had met in Mondon in his bar only a few weeks back.

After I was finished at the solicitor's office I was taken back to my hotel and had the rest of the day off. Court was at 9:00 a.m. the next morning and I would be collected at 8:30 a.m.

I must admit I was nervous but I was sure of my case so I had nothing to worry about. I think I have seen too many films where the lawyers tear the private investigator to bits in the witness box but I was confident I would be OK and the waiting time, as we all know, is the worst.

On arriving at the court buildings I was taken into a small room where I was instructed to wait and not speak to anybody. I waited about two hours before the solicitor came in and said that the court would be ready for me in a few minutes, and please remember to call the judge 'Sir', not 'Judge' or 'Your Honour', the solicitor said to me.

When my time came I was called to take my place at the back of the court. I immediately saw and recognised Mr. B sitting down in the front row with his legal team. He had not seen me and I wonder if he would recognise me, as I was wearing shorts and a T-shirt on my visit to his bar and now I had my black Johnny Cash suit on.

There was a silence in the court as I was asked to come forward to give evidence. As I walked forward I saw the face of Mr. B. He was white as a sheep and clearly in shock as he realised who I was; and I must admit I felt a little triumph over this little fat arrogant man.

The court usher came over to me and asked what religion I was and I said Christian. He then asked me to repeat the oath with my hand on the bible to tell the truth, the whole truth and nothing but the truth. "I do," I said.

The judge asked me to look at a paper that was a signed report from me and asked if I had written this report. I answered, "Yes sir I wrote and signed this report."

The judge asked Mr. B's lawyer if she had any questions for me. The female lawyer stood up immediately to start her cross examination, being the defense lawyer for Mr. B. She asked how long had I been a private investigator and if I knew Mrs. B before this case?

I replied that I had been a private investigator for many years in Spain and I did not know Mrs. B before this case.

Mr. Branson's lawyer asked me in a very sarcastic tone.

"Mr. Howatson, how long have been tapping the telephones of my client."

(As if I had been tapping the telephones of Mr. B to be able to set him up, and to be at the house that had just been sold at the exact same time that the couple that had bought the house came out.)

I replied that I had at no time interfered with the telephone of Mr. B and that it is illegal in Spain to do so, and secondly it was really by sheer coincidence that I was at the address supplied by the Spanish Land Registry at the time it was being sold, and that all the information that I had included in my report had been given to me voluntarily from Mr. B himself and his employee Jerry.

At that moment I looked at Mr. B straight in the eyes and he knew he was done for. His lawyer had no more to say as I had said it all. The judge then said, "If there are no further questions I will release the witness from his duty."

I was then asked to leave the court room. I went outside and back into the room that I was waiting in before. After 30 minutes or so an assistant of Mrs. B's solicitor came in and invited me for coffee.

I said, "That's the best news I have heard all day."

As we walked out into the hallway I saw Mr. B walking off with his lawyers, his hands in the air, mumbling some thing under his breath; at the same time he looked at me with eyes that could kill. But I never saw him again after that, thank goodness...

Later that day I was invited to a fantastic dinner with Mrs. B and her family (except for Mr. B) and then I was taken back to my hotel. Early the next morning, I was collected from my hotel and taken back to Gatwick Airport, my job now done and in good time to catch my return flight back to Spain.

It was a few weeks after I had returned to Spain that I was informed that Mrs. B had won her case against Mr. B, hands down and on all counts. Once again I was congratulated on the evidence that I had provided. My invoices were paid promptly without question and I was a happy bunny.

15

Protection and Extortion Rackets Rampant in Marbella — for the Aged, Weak and Vulnerable

Now this is really a very sad and disgusting case that I was asked by a very well known Spanish criminal lawyer Mr. Fernandez in Marbella, to investigate.

"Why me and not a Spanish private investigator?" I asked.

"No one else wanted the job," was the answer.

This made me curious to find out what this was all about. So off I went to Marbella, another six hours drive again from Cartagena, to meet the Spanish lawyers. Once I arrived at the lawyer's office in the old town area of Marbella I was faced with the problem of parking my trusty car. Normally I could leave my 12-year-old VW Golf anywhere, and even if the keys were in it nobody would want to steal it. They would most likely have pity on the owner and would think that it wouldn't drive anyway, and it certainly could not be used as a getaway car.

Well being fair to my rather old, well very old car that had over 380,000 thousand miles on the clock; it had served me well over the years. Sometimes the parking fees were more than the car was worth but it was a great under-cover car; I just had to be careful that it was not be towed away to the local rubbish tip.

I parked in an underground car park, hoping that I would not have to pay a deposit to come back and collect my car again. I often crack jokes about my old car, but I loved it just the same. I found the lawyer's office and went into the reception, where to my surprise in English, a very pretty lady said,

"Hello, sir! How can I help you?" (I wondered if she would have been so polite if she had seen the state of my car that I had just arrived in.)

"I am here to see Mr. Fernandez the lawyer; he should be expecting me," I said.

"What is your name sir?"

"Rick," I answered, hoping she would ask me out on a date!

"Please wait just a moment and Mr. Fernandez will be with you shortly."

Two minutes later the large teak wooden door opened and I was greeted with a hand shake from a middle aged very well dressed Spanish gentlemen.

"Thank you so much for coming, Rick, please come in my office," the lawyer said.

I went with him into his very impressive office like an obedient dog.

"Can I get you a drink?" the lawyer said.

I replied a cup of tea would be very nice and he pressed on his intercom and spoke to Miss Pretty and asked her to please bring in some tea.

"How can I assist you, Mr. Fernandez," I said.

In reply he went straight into the case history.

Mr. Fernandez had a client, to be exact an old aged couple that had retired and moved from the UK and come to Spain to live out their last few years in peace, in a warmer climate. But things had not turned out as they had expected. They bought themselves a very nice three-bedroom villa with a small swimming pool in the mountains of Marbella; truly a beautiful, picturesque site.

However once they had moved and had settled in after the stress of moving house the couple were naturally looking forward to the peace and quiet that their new home had to offer. But then the ugly side of moving to Spain raised its ugly face and the couple started to receive threatening telephone calls.

The calls were spoken all in English with an East London accent, from a person saying that he only wanted to help them. At first the couple ignored the telephone calls and did not report them to the police. But then they received a letter bomb posted into their letter box at the entrance of the small driveway to their house. Now the couple was petrified of what could happen next and did not know which way to turn. They came to the lawyer who had arranged the closing of the sale for their house, to ask his advice as they trusted his judgment.

The couple told that they had been instructed to pay 3,000 Euros monthly protection money to the anonymous telephone caller, to get the protection that they needed.

And if they did not the next bomb would be placed in their car, and the next in their new peaceful home, and so on.

"What can we do Rick?" the lawyer asked. "The police have no evidence to go on and do not want to get involved. Other private investigators in Malaga do not want to get involved either, as this looks very much like the Mafia; but which mafia? Could this be the English, Italian or Russian Mafia?"

I said that I would be prepared to look into the case but I would most likely need to bring in some heavyweights if the case was to go ahead. I knew some English private investigators up in Julio that were not only physical heavyweights, they were officially licensed to carry weapons in Spain. When the lawyer said he was happy with this arrangement, I said to start I would need a retainer. The lawyer said that he would have to speak to his clients first but could I please start to make enquiries so that I could give him an estimate of what my fees were likely to be; I agreed.

Then the lawyers' secretary Miss Pretty finally came in with the tea! I thought that she had to go to China for it. She apologised for the long wait, saying that normally clients would always drink coffee and that I was the first to ask for tea so she had to run down to the shop and buy some tea bags. I drank my tea down and before leaving the office I asked Mr. Fernandez if I could use his telephone in the reception as I had to make a few calls regarding the other agents to be involved, to see if they were available.

"No problem my secretary will help with anything you may need Rick," the lawyer replied.

My fantasies were running overtime!

I thought, "Yeah right". I wish Miss Pretty knew that she had the most beautiful body that you could imagine on a woman.

As we went into the reception she said, "Are you really a private detective?

"Well, er, yes," I said.

"Oh, that must be so exciting. Do you need an assistant?"

"Are you available?" I said.

"Well if my husband Mr. Fernandez would only let me go, then yes."

I decided *not* to go down that road and just smiled.

"May I use your phone please?"

"Of course help yourself. Just dial "0" to get an outside line."

Time to Call in the Heavies!

I telephoned Daniel, my buddy up in Julio, for some help. He answered the phone.

"Hi Daniel, I need at least five men for a job in Malaga; armed and available to travel as soon as possible and a ballpark figure of costs involved please buddy."

"Hello my friend," Daniel said. "Armed men will cost you fifteen hundred Euros per man per day, plus expenses, from the moment they leave base."

"Thanks buddy," I said and gave Inga a short briefing of the facts of the case.

"Looks like a bad one," Daniel said. "But if we are going to deal with it we will need at least three days notice to do some ground work. If the job is a go then I will need a retainer upfront of at least twenty thousand Euros, non refundable." I agreed, at the same time calculating how much I was going to charge for my part in the operation.

I left the lawyer's office and while I was waiting for a reply and instructions to proceed, I decided to make some local enquiries at the estate agent where the clients bought their house.

I was surprised to see that the sales manager was a Russian. I said that I was looking for a property for my old age parents to purchase. I enquired how many people worked in the estate agency and if they were all Russian as well. No, he told me, all the staff is English except for him. The owner of the agency ran a big agency in the United Kingdom in the City of London and potential clients would mostly come from there.

I said that my parents had friends that had already purchased a property in Marbella and that they were coming over to visit them and at the same time wanted to view a house in the same area. Out came all the pictures, and promises that they had the best thing since sliced bread. He was a good salesman but that was all; so I thanked him and said that I would have a look around and give him a call when my parents arrived.

I then wanted to speak with the couple that had received the letter bomb. Mr. Fernandez the criminal lawyer had given me their mobile telephone number so I gave them a call.

"Hello, I am a friend of Mr. Fernandez in Marbella and I need to speak to you."

"What is your name?"

"Rick," I replied.

We do not know you or anyone with that name Fernandez, what do you want to speak to us for?"

The poor people were obviously scared out of their minds.

"Look I think it would be better if I could meet you. Please telephone Mr. Fernandez, your lawyer, and he will explain what is going on," I said.

The phone went dead.

I telephoned the lawyer again, saying that I needed him to speak to the clients and would he please call them and arrange a meeting in the Orange Square in the old town of Marbella in an hour's time; then call me back and confirm it. He agreed. I waited for his return call.

In the meantime I walked around the 'old town' of Marbella. What a wonderful shopping centre — if you had money — I thought.

I saw the Rolex watch shop advertising watches for thousands of Euros and saw through the window a rather large security guard, standing just inside the entrance to the shop with an equally large baseball bat in his hand.

After 30 minutes or so I received a telephone call from Mr. Fernandez. It was now 5:00 p.m. and the couple would meet me at 6:30 when it was dark in the square, by the Tourist Information Centre.

"Thanks very much I hope to get back to you in the morning with a quotation," I said and I then informed Mr. Fernandez that I would be staying the night in Hostel Enrique just off Orange Square and that he could contact me on my mobile phone.

I checked in at the Hostel Enrique. It's not a youth hostel, as I certainly would not qualify for that anymore and would most likely get arrested if I tried to enter one; but having said that, I don't think that there are any youth hostels any more! Anyway, Hostel Enrique is more of a two-star cheap hotel, but fine for what I wanted. The underground parking was nearly the same price as the hostel, but I had to take care of my old jalopy, otherwise it would be a long walk home.

At 6:30 p.m. I was standing outside the tourist office when I recognised the two senior citizens that were to be my clients; as they very unconvincingly tried to make out that they were interested in the closed tourist office that had just closed for the night.

I approached them and said, "Hello; my name is Rick. Shall we have a coffee and a chat?"

I saw that their hands were shaking and shyly they nodded in agreement. We sat down inside the small restaurant as the couple did not want to be seen outside the restaurant with me; the restaurant was just off the Orange Square, with many others. The couple did not want anything to drink but I said that if we sit in a restaurant we have to order something, so they asked for a glass of red wine and I ordered coffee; I just love the Spanish coffee.

"Please," I said, "I know you have had a rough ride and a horrific experience and I am here to help you; but I need to know all that you can tell me about when and how you bought your house and who else knew about it."

At first they were reluctant to discuss what had happened to them, out of fear of retribution, but once they did start I couldn't get a word in edgeways. The paper trail led to the estate agency in Marbella and then to the estate agent in the UK.

I now knew enough to start working out a plan of action. I thanked them for coming to see me and said that if there was any change in the situation to call me or Mr. Fernandez at once. Before leaving I asked one last question. "Why did you not report this to the police?"

The frail old man looked at me and said they had tried to but nobody spoke English. I said that would most likely be the same if you were in the UK and you communicated with the police in Spanish; they would need you to speak in English! That didn't go down too well at all.

The old lady looked at me and asked how much it was all going to cost them. I said that I would have to speak to Mr. Fernandez and he would inform them, as I would be officially be working for him, so that there would be no connection between me and them for security reasons.

8:00 p.m. — I walked back to the Hostel Enrique and straight to my room and started working on a plan. The costs would be high if I had to bring in five men through Daniel, so I worked on having just two for starters, plus myself. The question of the day was even if we did find enough evidence to convict these louts, would this stop the protection racket? Or would another group just carry on where the other left off? Could we even bust what was looking like an international crime ring? Had I bitten off too much this time? And with that I went to sleep.

The next morning I woke up and went out to get some coffee as you could not get anything to eat or drink in the hostel; it was a sleep only joint. As I was sitting in a breakfast bar I was looking at the hundreds of people walking about and it was only 9:00 in the morning. In my little village near Cartagena you would never see so many people in a whole month, except during the tourist season.

I had a quote ready for Mr. Fernandez for one weeks work, being ten hours a day and seven days a week for three armed agents. In total 35,000 Euros; this would include all expenses. I know this was expensive but we were putting our lives on the line here and no amount of money is worth a bullet in the head.

I was thinking about the Madeline MacCann case in Portugal where the Spanish private investigators billed £50,000 a month for trying to find who had abducted poor little Madeline and to bring her home! They did jack shit — and no guns or physical violence was involved.

10:00 a.m. In the morning — I telephoned Mr. Fernandez and spoke to Miss Pretty.

"My husband does not come in the office till one o'clock as he is in court," she told me.

"Thanks very much. Please ask him to call me on my mobile, as I need to speak to him rather urgently," I said.

"I will of course," replied Miss Pretty.

I checked out of the hostel and put my little overnight bag in my car and started my return trip home, wondering when would the glamour of being a private investigator set in, if ever...

It was now 4:00 p.m. in the afternoon and I was already driving past the region of Almeria; only another 200 clicks to go when my telephone rang.

"Hello how can I help you?"

"Hello Rick, this is Pedro Fernandez returning your call."

"Hi Mr. Fernandez, One moment; I need to pull over for a minute," I said, as I did not have a hands free telephone set in my car.

"How much is your quotation and how do you suggest we should go forward from here?" Mr. Fernandez said.

"Well we could start the work in three days but I would need a non-refundable retainer of five thousand Euros and a total of fifteen thousand Euros, for two agents for seven days. If three armed agents are needed it will be a total of thirty-five thousand Euros."

"There is of course no guarantee that we will get a conviction or to be honest with you that we can stop the racketeering, unless the police help us all the way." The phone was silent.

"Hello Mr. Fernandez are you still there?"

"Er yes, I am still listening," Mr. Fernandez said.

"Well that is what I wanted to tell you Mr. Fernandez," I said.

"Well Rick, thank you very much. It does sound very expensive though."

I explained in detail how I had calculated the costs and said that I would get my secretary to send him a written quotation just as soon as I had returned back in to my office. (I just wish I *had* a bloody secretary, and that I had charged for the consultation in Marbella.)

It was dark when I arrived home and I just wanted to sleep but I needed money more; so I looked at my notes and got to work on my little laptop. In the early hours of the morning I was finished at last and I emailed Mr. Fernandez a really nice professional quotation, also thanking him for his time and advising that I was looking forward to receiving his instructions, and the retainer to start the job.

I was really not prepared for the reply that I received a few hours later.

"Dear Rick thank you for coming to Marbella to discuss this case with me. Unfortunately, I have since been informed by my clients that they have since reached an agreement with the protection gang. They, my clients, only have to pay a thousand Euros a month now to the gangsters, instead of three thousand Euros, and they will be protected. My clients have accepted this offer."

Now that I really did not expect to hear what I was about to be told and was shocked to say the least. But, you win some and you lose some.

When employing the services of a private investigator instead of saying, "I cannot afford to go ahead," one should really think first whether you can really afford *not* to go ahead.

I thanked the lawyer and said if he needed me in the future he now knew how to contact me. That was it, the end of an uneventful story.

To be lonely, scared and not being able to trust anyone is one of the saddest things of our time. And these people came to Spain to live out their days with a better quality of life in the sunshine. I wish them luck and may God bless them.

16

The Mallorca Cocaine Case

This case came from an agency in London that really wanted to dump a client on to me so that they could be rid of him. It did not take too long to find out why.

The case was to trace the ex-wife of a client and to gather evidence of her using cocaine and introducing her 14-year-old daughter to the habit. The London-based agent asked me to telephone Jon the client in Mallorca and to deal with him directly.

I spoke to my new client Jon, who lived in a very elite area of Mallorca, not too far from the fishing village of Cala Ratijada, a fun place for the people that can afford it. Jon was a small Englishman in his early 60's and was very excited and wanted two agents to start at once working in Mallorca at once.

The instructions seemed easy enough to follow but the big problem was that it was the high season. The small Island of Mallorca had over 3 million visiting tourists, all wanting a bit of the Spanish sunshine and a good holiday. Of course all the prices were up threefold, as in all the tourist resorts in Spain, and it was very difficult to get flights and a hotel and hire a car at such short notice as everything was booked up. But we managed it in the end, with the help of Ann, our agent on the ground. Ann had lived in Mallorca for years and was very astute at getting things done. Soon all was organised and we were on our way flying from Alicante to Palma de Mallorca; within two days of even knowing about the case; not bad going.

On arrival in Palma, I contacted our ground agent, who came to meet Inga and me at the airport and drove us to our hotel. Ann had done the ground work on the case, and pointed out the bars as we drove past them, and the address of the client. Once we arrived at our hotel I telephoned the client to make arrangements to meet him in a restaurant not far from his house.

Strangely he seemed surprised that we were on the island, and said that he did not expect us. This was of course nonsense, as I had informed him of every move I was making and if there was any uncertainty then I would not have gone to all the trouble to be there in the first place.

Jon was a typical choleric personality. He stood 5 foot 3 inches short, and had a big diamond stud in his ear, like David Beckham. Not really what we expected to see.

"I have employed two detectives from New Scotland Yard to fly over and do the job," Jon said to me. I was getting annoyed now and when Jon saw the expression in my face he said, "Well they have not arrived yet, so I suppose you had better take their place."

"Jon before we go any further I need the retainer that we spoke about on the telephone when you confirmed that we should come," I said.

Now Jon did not seem to have a very good memory but I pushed for the retainer anyway. Jon looked puzzled. "I do not have that kind of money on me," he said, hoping that I would believe him.

"OK Jon," I said. "We will be going straight back to the airport and flying home to mainland Spain and sending our invoice to the agents in London." Jon accepted that he was beat and said that he had the cash in his house, and was ready to pay the 6,000 Euros that was the agreed retainer.

Jon wanted surveillance carried out in a night club bar where his ex-wife was having an affair with the manager of the club, where she was probably also snorting cocaine in the club with her under-aged daughter.

I informed Jon that we needed first to establish where his ex-wife was living in the village, as Jon did not know himself, and then to observe her movements in the evening. Jon's ex-wife did not live alone; she had her 14-year-old daughter Susannah from her marriage with Jon with her. Susannah wanted nothing to do with her father for whatever reason — which we did not know at the time.

I told Jon that he would have to back off and let us do our job but I was now getting to understand why the English agents were so keen to dump Jon on to me. I think in all honesty what Jon really wanted would be to march into the night club with a machine gun, and shoot everybody in sight, including his wife and daughter.

Jon was becoming a problem; he was a friendly rogue but a bloody pest, to say the least and followed me around like a dog.

Inga and I went with Jon to collect the retainer from his house. Did I just say 'house'? No; this was not a normal house; this was a beautiful two million pound villa, and situated in a picturesque private bay, very secluded. Jon had the Mediterranean Sea in his back garden, with private access. We were so impressed with Jon's house; but Jon seemed to take it all for granted. He lived alone and all the time he had nothing better to do than to badmouth his wife to us.

He told Inga and me a story of how he was set up by his wife in their house in London. Jon visited his wife, to try and come to an amicable agreement over the divorce settlement; but he made the stupid mistake of going alone to the house where his wife lived.

The amicable agreement very quickly turned into a heated debate that ended up with Jon threatening to kill his wife. Only in court did Jon find out that his daughter was in the house all the time, hiding in a wardrobe, tape recording all the swearing and threats from Jon to his wife. A restraining order was granted to Jon's ex-wife against Jon, stopping him from coming within 300 yards of her and her daughter. He would be arrested if he violated that court order.

I could not understand Jon. He obviously had lots of money, so why did he not just let some slick city lawyer deal with the divorce settlement? Instead Jon wanted to do everything himself and make the situation so much worse.

The plot continues.

Jon gave me the retainer. As it was getting late, I said that we would start first thing in the morning. Inga and I walked back to the hotel that Ann had reserved for us.

Back in the hotel we looked at our options and they were not too good. First thing in the morning we would try and locate Jon's ex-wife but we needed a starting point. We knew where she would be in the evenings; according to Jon, his wife would be in the Angel Night Club with her lover every night. But that was when she was visiting Mallorca, and we were not certain if she was on the island or not. Jon said he thought she was. Normally she lived in London. She had divorced him two years ago; but Jon just could not let go.

The next morning after breakfast Inga and I started hunting around the village at the breakfast bars. Ann joined us for the day and we managed with local enquiries to establish where Jon's ex-wife was living with her daughter. They were currently on the island, but only for a few more days. I decided to keep this information to myself, until I knew what Jon was capable of.

We had been running around all day and as it was Thursday the night club was closed. Friday and Saturday were the busy nights of the week for the clubs. We carried out surveillance of the night clubs and took loads of photographs. We had earned some peace and quiet by then so we returned to our hotel and then enjoyed a few hours in the sunshine by the hotel pool. Jon was telephoning me every half an hour for updates, and he was now really becoming a nuisance and getting in the way of things.

Friday night was to be an all-nighter in the club. Inga went into the night club on her own and I waited outside in a hired car. Our two-way radios were not good enough quality to use and rather obvious, so we kept in contact through our mobile phones. I could see Inga clearly through the front bay windows of the night club. It was strange for a night club to have windows; but there again it was a holiday resort and not a night club as we would know them in big cities like London or New York.

The barman had taken a fancy to Inga and gave her free Coca-Cola all night. As I saw Inga dancing I could also see at least three drug dealers clearly outside the club, peddling drugs. The law was of course nowhere to be seen. I went into the club to check things out and it was full of youngsters and a few older couples but I really felt out of place; I mean this was just not my scene at all. The music was so loud that I could not even hear the dealers asking me if I wanted a fix.

I lasted ten minutes inside and then went back to the car. Poor Inga, I thought; but she was enjoying every minute of it and she fitted in perfectly. At the bar was Jon's ex and his 14-year-old daughter, both drinking Bacardi and Coke and busy talking with some young men. We found out that Jon's ex-wife had invested money into the bar and was a 50% owner.

The evening turned into morning and there was a constant coming and going of youngsters, but Jon's ex-wife and daughter stayed on in the club.

3:45 a.m. — Inga went to the ladies room in the club, walking in as Jon's ex-wife was busy snorting cocaine. She did not try to hide or cover up what she was doing; the lady was so sure of herself and did not seemed to be concerned about anything; but there again she was high.

Inga called me and reported what was going on. Jon's daughter was now a little drunk and falling about on the dance floor with a Spanish guy about ten years older than her.

4 am — I decided to abort the surveillance because things were getting too messy and if the cops did a hit on the night club then we certainly did not want to be involved with drug issues that were going on. We had witnessed Jon's ex-wife taking drugs, witnessed their 14-year-old daughter drinking alcohol and staying out all night in the bar, and as a minor this was of course illegal, unethical and immoral.

As Inga came out of the night club the barman was close on her tail. The barman invited Inga to go out with him to another night club but Inga declined and he was very disappointed.

"Maybe another day," she said, to spare his feelings.

Inga joined me in the hired car and was reporting all that she had seen, when a head popped up by the passenger's window. I could not believe my eyes; it was Jon sneaking around on his knees by the side of my car.

"Jon," I said, "what are you doing here?"

"I just came to see what's going on. They are in there, aren't they?"

"Jon please; you will blow everything if anybody sees you with us," I said, but Jon seemed unable to hear. "Jon please go back home we will report back to you later," I said. "Let it go. We will come to your house, but please go now."

Finally, like a little hunchback, Jon sneaked off into the darkness of the night again.

At that moment the daughter came out with a young man and the two of them got onto a motorcycle and drove off into the same direction that Jon had just taken. So we had to tail them to make sure that they did not run into Jon and have a confrontation.

Luckily for everyone, Jon had taken a short cut to his house across a field, so he never saw that his daughter half drunk, was on the back of a motorcycle, most probably on her way to get laid by the young man she was riding with.

At 5:00 in the morning, Inga and I went back to our hotel to get some well earned sleep.

10:00 a.m. and Jon was calling me!

"Where is the report and pictures from last night? Was she in the bar all night? I am sure she was."

"Jon, please give me a chance, we have been up all night."

No answer.

"Yes she was there and your daughter," I told him, "but I could not see the boyfriend make any advances to her at all, he spoke to her a couple of times and bought drinks for her but nothing more."

I was worried about what to tell Jon because he was so unstable. He was clearly not satisfied with what I had to tell him but I thought it for the best at that moment. I said that we could meet up later for a coffee in one of the hotel bars at midday; he agreed and hung up.

I telephoned the agents in London and asked them for more history on the case and what Jon did in London before he took early retirement.

It transpired that Jon was a second-hand car dealer from Chelsea. Well that made a few things clear as to his wealth. The agent apologised for putting Jon onto me, as they had had experiences with him in London which were not good; but he paid.

I explained the case and asked for advice. The agent advised that I would have to inform him of what was going on as he was the client, but to delay the written report until I was back in mainland Spain in my office. That sounded like good advice to me. I then talked it over with Inga and she agreed.

I met Jon at midday for coffee and I could see he was nearly going to explode if I did not have something more to tell him.

"Jon, the instructions you gave me were to locate where your ex-wife is living and that has been done. Agreed? She is living with your daughter Susannah. We will send you the address once we have confirmed it with our data base, which will be next Monday. We confirmed that your wife and daughter were in the Angels Night Club until the early hours of this morning. Agreed? We could not confirm that she is having an affair with the night club owner, but we can confirm that your ex-wife legally bought fifty percent ownership of the night club two months ago. Now that is where we stand to-date." Jon nodded his little bald head in agreement.

I made the mistake of trying to talk sense into Jon; but it had no effect on him. Jon demanded that we spend another night in the night club on surveillance. I was not happy about it but it was a job so I agreed on the condition that Jon had to stay away from the bar; reluctantly he agreed. Jon went back to his mansion and I chilled out with Inga by the hotel swimming pool.

After dinner it was time to start work; the night club opened its doors at 10:00 p.m. As Inga and I drove past there was not one punter in the club so we drove on into the village and went for a walk. It was a beautiful summer evening and I was not looking forward to sitting in the car all night. I would far sooner be in the car than in the noisy smoke filled night club.

At 1:00 a.m. we returned. Inga went inside the club and I went to my observation point, where I could keep my eye on Inga. The barman was very happy to see Inga and thought she had come back just to see him; and I think Inga enjoyed the attention she was getting.

Jon's ex-wife propped up the bar and was already quite merry with her Bacardi and Coke. Nothing much had changed except that Susannah was not to be seen anywhere and there was a large number of men sitting around, as if they were waiting for somebody or something to happen. Again I could clearly see the drug dealers at work outside the club.

At 2:45 Jon's ex-wife went to the ladies room, followed by Inga. As Inga entered the ladies room she could see Jon's ex-wife snorting her cocaine again. Inga did not stay; she washed her hands and came out and called me asking what to do? "That's it," I said, "let's go home. Abort and come out of the club."

Inga and I sat in the car and would you believe it, a drug dealer came up to our parked car and asked if we needed anything!

"No, we are fine thanks," I said.

We waited outside the club till 4:30 a.m. when the barman came out to lock up, and we saw Jon's ex-wife stumble out and get into a white Mini Cooper; it looked as if one of the bar girls was giving her a spin home.

We followed the Mini Cooper at a distance and watched as the car stopped outside of the little white house that we had located on our first day working on the case. The lights were still on and Jon's ex-wife got out of the car and went inside the little house on her own.

6:00 a.m. next morning it was broad daylight, with the sun coming up in the east. Inga and I went to Jon's villa to give a verbal report to him. He had of course telephoned me several times during the night demanding updates .

I said to Jon that our work was now finished and that we would be flying back to mainland Spain in four hour's time. I reported to him all that we had seen and said that our pictures would have to be down loaded on the computer to see if they were of any use, as it was very dark inside the club.

I told Jon that now he knew everything that we had witnessed, including the cocaine snorting and that his daughter was drinking all night in the club. He would get a detailed written report once I had returned to my office.

"Jon," I pleaded, "please do not lose your cool now. Do not telephone your ex-wife as it will only mean trouble. And for God's sake do not go near the night club, as it looks like a set-up."

"OK, OK, OK!" Jon said.

As we got up to leave, he was already on the telephone screaming abuse at his ex-wife. Inga I left him at his mansion and drove directly to Palma Airport, gave back the hire car and went into the departure terminal.

We caught our flight back to mainland Spain and there must have been a million other people at the airport wanting to travel at the same time. It was quite a fight to get through the crowds, but it was worth it to get home again, to our little laid-back village near Cartagena.

I took Inga home. Now I needed a couple of days rest from the job in Mallorca, but there was other work that had come in on my computer. First I started writing the ten-page report for Jon.

The next day I received a telephone call from a man saying that he was an ex-Scotland Yard detective and that Jon had called him as he was in trouble.

"How can I help?" I said.

"I need your report in the form of an affidavit so that it can be produced in court," he answered.

"Sorry I cannot help you. Jon is the only person that I am authorised to take instructions from and give information to."

The ex-Scotland Yard detective was not happy with my reply.

"Jon has been arrested and is in prison!" he informed me.

"Oh I am sorry to hear that, but to be honest, not surprised. Please ask Jon to contact me through his solicitor and I will do what I can."

Jon called me six weeks later saying that he had been set up. As he entered the night club he was jumped by four men and beaten up. There were ten witnesses that testified in court that Jon entered the night club and immediately attacked his ex-wife and that the four men had to restrain Jon until the police arrived and arrested him in the Angels Night Club.

Jon was of course found guilty in court. The judge handed him a nine-month prison sentence in a Spanish jail — a far cry from his luxury mansion.

There was no appeal made against Jon's sentence and a new restraining order was made from the Spanish court barring him for five years of going within 500 metres of his ex-wife or daughter.

Jon's biggest enemy is himself and although I do feel sorry for him, he deserves all he got. I am sorry Jon, but it's true.

17

My New Secondhand Work Horse

Although things were not looking good for Jon, things had got better for me and I persuaded myself to buy a new car. My old VW Golf had served me well and after 14 years it was time to say goodbye. I was attached to my ole car and my emotions ran high when I received replies to the advert that I had placed in one of the free English newspapers. I had put my car up for sale for 1,000 Euros. In England I would have had to pay to have the car collected and taken away, but the second hand car market is good in Spain.

After speaking with several potential buyers I agreed to meet a buyer to negotiate the price, although there really was no room for negotiation. A man in his late 50's arrived with his son, who was 19 years old with piercings in his eyebrow, nose and bottom lip, plus earrings in both ears. I am sorry, I am old fashioned, but earrings on a man — yuck. I was a bit envious of his long hair though, but altogether he was a scruffy bastard and I was not happy that he would be the new owner of my faithful 'Folks Wagon', as it was the boy's father that was paying for the car. I swallowed my emotions as the car had to go to make room for the new second-hand car that I wanted to buy. So my dear old VW was sold for 900 Euros.

I was sad to see my old car disappear down the road. Even sadder when I was telephoned a couple of weeks later by the boy's father telling me that his son had crashed the car and it was a write-off. That was a terribly sad end for such a trusted old friend.

May my Golf rest in peace...

My new car was a BMW 320 diesel saloon car, two years old and only 75,000 miles on the clock. It was like new but it did have one embarrassing problem and that was with the central locking system. When the weather was really hot and the sun was beating down on the car, the central locking refused to function and so the only door that would open would be the driver's door. I visited four different BMW specialists, service and repair centres up and down Spain. They said no problem; I just had to install a whole new central locking system — at a cost of 3,000 Euros.

When the mechanics came out to try the central locking system of course it worked, it was as if my car was having its own little private joke with me, known as 'taking the piss'. But once I had left the BMW garage and drove around the corner, the central locking refused to work again.

Luckily Inga was young and fit as she was the one that had to climb in and out of the car via the driver's window, to the amusement of many passersby.

18

The Story of Ramona

As I have already said process service is the bread and butter money for the private investigator such as myself, and we often had a lot of fun tracking down the people that had to be served and in most cases did not want the papers anyway.

Back in my office I received instructions to serve a freezing order on a very pretty redhead in her late twenties, an English lady. Her name was Ramona and she was in the middle of divorce proceedings back in the UK with her husband, after just three years of marriage. Ramona's husband came to a financial settlement with his ex-beloved before the divorce proceedings were actually concluded in the divorce courts. In his financial settlement he gave his wife £750,000 cash and as there were no children involved, he was to keep the family home in the UK; leaving his wife to move on with her new life with a very wealthy Indian restaurant owner in Spain

The problem reared its ugly head when the lawyers acting on behalf of Ramona, stated that the financial settlement had not been forthcoming, nor had it been agreed. The husband loved and trusted his lovely wife Ramona; and that is one thing that you just cannot afford to do when love turns to war.

The judge ordered that Ramona should be served with a 'freezing order' until it could be decided in court who was telling the truth. Then he would then act accordingly.

I received a nice picture of Ramona, her telephone number and the address of the Indian restaurant in Murcia. I first visited the Indian restaurant to see if luck would have it that Ramona was there, as I was informed that she did spend a lot of time there.

The restaurant was a single-storey, 90-seater upmarket Indian restaurant. The Indian staff were as friendly as one could expect, but not helpful. The staff knew Ramona but could not say when she would be back in the restaurant next and they did not know where she lived, even though she lived with their boss! The staff did not want to say anything, whether they knew or not; but I can understand saying the wrong thing could cost them their job.

I thanked them and left a note for Ramona to please call me as I had some important documents for her; but Ramona had absolutely no intention of calling or meeting me as she was aware of what documents I had for her.

My next move was to telephone Ramona on her mobile telephone number that had been supplied by the solicitors, and to my surprise she answered!

I immediately said, "Hello Ramona, I was in the restaurant today looking for you as I have some court documents for you."

"Who are you?" she said.

"Oh I am sorry; I do apologise. My name is Rick and I am a court process server, Ramona. I need to meet with you today please."

"Oh no I am sorry I am not available today; maybe at the end of the week."

"Ramona, can we meet at the Indian restaurant either today or tomorrow please."

"I will have to see. I will call you back. Give me your number."

I gave Ramona my telephone numbers but I somehow knew that she would not call me back. I wrote an interim report to my client updating and informing him that I had made contact with Ramona and that she was not very helpful.

Late that evening I telephoned Ramona again, asking for an appointment to meet her but she said that she did not have time to meet me and just hung the telephone up on me.

The next day I was pleased to receive a telephone call from my client saying that he had expected that Ramona would try and avoid service; but the latest news was that Ramona was flying back to England with Midland Air at 9:00 p.m. that very evening. So I could serve her at Murcia Airport in the departure lounge.

7:30 p.m. — Inga and I arrived at Murcia Airport and took up our places in the departure lounge. The queue for the Midland Air flight to London Gatwick had already started to form; but there was no sign of Ramona.

An hour passed and the queue got bigger and bigger but there was still no Ramona. Then at the same moment that the flight boarding was announced, Ramona arrived, with her Indian boyfriend carrying her bags like a trusty servant walking behind her.

Inga was busy taking the photos of the lovely Ramona as I approached her and said, "Hello Ramona."

Ramona was surprised to see me. With a big smile on her face and a little bit confused she blurted out, "Hello. How did you know that I was here?"

I ignored her question and offering the court documents said, "Ramona I am serving you with these courts orders," but before I could finish the sentence she pushed me to one side and said that she did not want them.

Her trusty Indian friend was just looking on in amazement as I said again to Ramona, "You are served," and put the documents down at her feet. I then walked away, leaving the papers of her private life being scattered and flying all over the departure lounge floor. A young lady from the air line staff picked the papers up and went running after Ramona. "Excuse me! Madam, I think you have dropped these papers."

Ramona said that they were not hers and just walked on, though her name was clear to see on the papers.

I saw Ramona and her boyfriend walk over to airport security and I think that they were complaining about me. Just then, to my very pleasant surprise, loud and clear over the airport loud speaker system in the departure lounge was heard: "Attention, Attention. Would Mrs. Ramona Smith please report to the departure lounge counter and collect her papers please."

Ramona looked around in astonishment. And even though she had been beat, would you believe it, in court she denied receiving the court orders! But then the defense lawyer handed the judge the photographs that Inga took of Ramona in the airport departure lounge, along with my sworn affidavit.

Ramona had nowhere to run and lost her case.

19

Process Service in Ibiza

The solicitors or agents who supply me with work, often say a particular process service will be "an easy job." They never say: "Be careful; you could get a smack in the mouth as this person to be served just really does not want to see you!"

I always ask for the address of the person to be served, so that I check it out if it's a genuine house address, or a bus stop, before I can give the clients a quote. Most clients do not understand the problems we have here in Spain, trying to find people that do not want to be found. It is never just a straightforward delivery of court documents.

I once received a process service for an English male resident, "somewhere on the Island of Ibiza." Ibiza is one of the three Balearic Islands, which attracts more tourists than all the other islands in the Mediterranean put together. But in the off season, Ibiza is like a scary, grey coloured graveyard, with over 90% of the hotels, clubs and bars closed for the winter months.

The documents to be served seemed a straightforward divorce order of the court and the address looked OK — until I arrived in Ibiza.

I drove up to the Port of Denia from Murcia and then travelled by the inter-island ferry boat service, across to the first stop, which was Ibiza. It was an eight-hour sea crossing and by the time I arrived in Ibiza it was already late afternoon.

I disembarked from the ferry boat and walked over to the taxi stand and waited 15 minutes for a taxi. When the taxi arrived he drove me to a cheapish hotel that had rooms available, as most of the tourist accommodations were closed for the winter months. I checked in to the hotel and then made enquiries about the address that I needed to visit. I then instructed the taxi driver to get me as near as possible to the address of the target that I had to process serve.

I was looking for a bar called 'Joey's Ark' that was on the beach front. Being the low season, most of all the bars and restaurants were also closed. Every time I saw a light on in a building I hurried towards it, hoping somebody would be there that could assist me with my enquiries and tell me where the bar was that I was looking for, or if they had they heard of an Englishman named Lester.

But I was to be out of luck for some time yet as nobody knew the bar, or the Englishman.

It was now 1:00 in the morning and I was really dead tired of walking, and frustrated. I had obviously come at the wrong time of year to be able to get my man. So I started the long walk back to the hotel, as there were no taxis at that time in the morning.

As I plodded on, I saw an Irish bar with lights on and I could hear people inside, so I thought I would chance my luck and ask one more time. The barman — a large, black bearded Spaniard — (what else to expect in an Irish bar?) was getting ready to close the bar.

I asked the barman in Spanish if he knew of Joey's Bar and he said no, but the English people over there in the corner by the door would know. My luck was picking up and now with new hope I addressed the group of English speaking people, who actually sounded Welsh, and were all half drunk.

"Hi there good people. Would any of you know Joey's bar run by an Englishman called Lester?" I said in a very tired voice.

Nobody had heard of the bar or of Lester Smith. But just I was about to leave a lady in her mid 60's spoke up.

"Just a minute, you mean Lisa's place don't you? Her partner is Les or Lester and they have a little bar on the sea front."

"Yes," I said. "That could be them."

"I can show you where it is, if you wait a couple of minutes," she offered.

"That would be great," I said.

I waited for the woman by the doorway of the bar, watching her down pints of Guinness. When she was ready to leave she could hardly stand up straight, but beckoned me to follow her. As the cold night air hit her in the face she mumbled something like it was on her way home. I thought it very strange that this woman would be so trusting, as I was a complete stranger to her.

We stumbled on through the unlit streets and the time was now 2:00 a.m. We walked for about 25 minutes and I was wondering where the hell the old lady was taking me and maybe it was me that was too trusting. At this point in time the old lady was leaning on me so, I was half carrying her.

Then she said, "There you are! That's Joey's Bar right here, but it's closed."

"Well I was hardly expecting it to be open in the low season at two thirty in the morning," I replied.

"Lisa and Les don't live here you know," the old lady said. "And who are you anyway and what do you want from them?"

I said that I was a friend of the family and I needed to inform Les of some sad news. The old lady then got her mobile telephone out and stumbled around punching in a number. I thought that whoever she was telephoning would not be pleased to receive a call at this time in the morning from an old lady, well on the way to being totally pissed.

"Sarah is that you?" the old lady muttered. "I need the telephone number for Lisa and Les. I know it's late but, well there's a man here who needs to speak to Les, because his mother has passed away!"

I immediately tried to get the attention of the old lady.

"That's not true at all," I told her.

"Write this number down," she replied and repeated a mobile

telephone number for Les Smith. Then she thanked her friend and put her mobile telephone back in her pocket.

"I did not say that his mother had passed away; how on earth could you say that? Maybe it's the wrong person altogether and they could be worried now, thinking that their mother has passed away."

The old lady took no interest at all in what I had to say and just mumbled, "You can take me home now."

The old lady now not only leaning all over me, she was starting to get tired and wanted to sleep, and every now and again she farted. I had to keep on reminding her to tell me where she lived, but thank goodness it was not too far to go.

After ten minutes she said, "I live here on my own; if you want to come in you can."

I said, "No thanks, I have to get home. My people will be worried about where I am so late at night."

That was the best excuse I could think of at the time.

It took me another thirty minutes to find my hotel and then to find my bed; I really needed my sleep now. I slept in till 11:00 the next morning and missed my breakfast, but I did not care; I was just too tired.

I looked for the telephone number and called the mobile number that the old lady had given to me. A female voice answered.

"Hi, this is Lisa."

"Hi, Lisa. Is Lester there please?" I said.

"Yeah. Who's calling?" she asked.

"It's Rick," I replied.

A minute later a man's voice came on. "Hello."

"Hi, is that Lester Smith?"

"It is! What can I do for you?"

"Lester my name is Rick. I am a court process server from the courts in England and I have been sent to Ibiza to meet you and give you some documents. This is very important for you; because if you do not respond to these court orders, then a judgment can be made in your absence."

Lester started to tell me his life story on the telephone and after a few minutes he agreed to meet me at a breakfast bar that was open on the main road in the town centre.

I went straight to the breakfast bar and had downed a club sandwich and an orange juice before Lester arrived. I could see most of the street from where I was sitting outside the restaurant. It was a nice warm day and then I saw who had to be Lester coming towards me, with two huge German shepherd dogs and a young lady half his age, next to him. He came up to me and I stood up and greeted the dogs first. (Lester could not know that I have had a lot of experience with this breed of dog and although they looked very intimidating the dogs were really friendly and docile.

Lester and his girlfriend sat down and we talked and at the same time I gave Lester the court orders. He started to bad mouth his ex-wife and all the bad things she had done to him and I just listened patiently, hoping it would not take all bloody day.

After Lester had quietened down a bit I reminded him that it was absolutely imperative that he give a written response to the courts. I then took my leave; wished him and his girlfriend good luck and made it back to my hotel in time to check out and catch the next ferry boat returning to the port of Denia, mainland Spain.

I was satisfied that I had accomplished my challenge successfully and arrived back home without further incident. I wrote my report and relaxed for two days, before my next job.

20

Kai's Long Swedish Fingers

Not all process serving is successful. Back in my office I received a telephone call from a solicitor in London. He had a very urgent court order that needed to be served — if possible 'the day before yesterday'.

"Do you have the address?" I asked.

"Well, we believe it is in Gerona," the solicitor replied.

"I am sorry, but in order to be able to help you, I will need a full postal address. Do you realise that Gerona is well over a thousand miles north of Cartagena, where I am based?"

The solicitor asked me to speak directly with his client — in other words, he didn't want to get involved. "Would you please liaise with our client? He knows more than we do at the moment."

"I will do what I can. Please ask your client to call me. And if I can do this work, I will need to have all instructions in writing, before I can confirm that I am able to do the job," I said.

The solicitor agreed and hung up.

Ten o'clock that evening the client, a Mr. O'Donnell, telephoned me, thanking me for agreeing to carry out the work.

"Hey hold on a minute, I have not agreed anything so far," I said. "We need to get some things clear first. With the distance involved and the time it will take, it will cost two thousand pounds to carry out this service; and before we go any further, I need your full details and the address of where the subject is to be served in Gerona."

Mr. O'Donnell told me that his ex-girlfriend, an air stewardess for British Airways, had disappeared with his son and that he believed that she was with an airline pilot from British Airways and living in Gerona. The court order was to return his son back to the jurisdiction of the UK and to his custody at once, as he was the custodial parent.

(It's always upsetting to see how adults behave when it comes to the kids, who of course are the victims and suffer the most in these custody battles.)

Mr. O'Donnell had an address in Gerona but was not a hundred percent certain that the subjects would be there. I said that I needed to get the instructions via email along with the documents that needed to be served; but first and foremost I needed an immediate transfer of £2,000, otherwise I could not proceed. I would leave for Gerona as soon as I received the above, if he was in agreement. He was in agreement.

To my surprise, shortly afterwards FedEx telephoned me, enquiring if they could deliver some urgent documents to me first thing in the morning. (This proves that the system can work some times.)

"Sure; I will be at home," I said.

I received the instructions by email and the original court orders by FedEx. I also received an email with the money transfer codes, to collect two payments of £1,000 from the Western Union office at my local post office in town.

Things were moving very fast.

I planned to leave in the evening and drive through the night to Gerona. Inga my partner was busy with other things and could not accompany me on this trip at such short notice.

I called in the help of a neighbour of mine, Kai from Sweden, who was holidaying in his summer house that was just opposite my apartment.

"Hi Kai, do you fancy a trip to the north of Spain and back, all expenses paid?" I asked.

"Oh yes, I would like that very much. Please may I come with you?" he answered.

I said OK and I was glad to have the company. Kai has been out on a couple of trips in the past with me and we had a good time. Kai's wife was not with him on his holiday as she had to stay and work back in Sweden. She is a social worker and was in charge of a drug rehabilitation unit for young addicts. That has got to be one of the worst jobs going and they were always short of staff to take care of the youngsters.

Let me tell you a little about my friend Kai from Sweden. Kai speaks a little English and when we are on the road, talking to pass the time, it's more like a television panel game; and yes he is the weakest link. He is two very impressive metres tall. Kai comes from a very remote part of West Sweden and is a policeman, as he has been for the past 30 years. Kai by his own admission would far sooner be a private investigator in Spain for the excitement, but he cannot give up his day job and I believe it is better that way…

I like Kai a lot and it is just as well because to do this job we will be in the car on the road for the next 24 or 48 hours, non-stop.

We left Cartagena City to travel the 1,500-kilometre trip up north and got lost a few times but nothing serious. We arrived in Gerona at 11:00 in the morning and Kai had been happily snoring most of the way. We had driven past Alicante, Valencia, Tarragona, Barcelona and were now only 40 miles from the French border and Gerona.

Now this is where the hunting really started.

The address was not very helpful, although the area was very picturesque with little houses dotted all over the mountainside, but it did not give us a real clue as to where the house was. It took a lot of leg work and most of the day till we eventually found the house where the targets were situated for the process service.

Kai took up his covert observation point with a camera at the ready. It is very important to photograph the subjects accepting or refusing acceptance of the court orders to submit as evidence to the court. A picture is better than a thousand words; well, sometimes.

My job was to try and lure the targets out of the house and to give them the court orders in full view of the camera. Kai's job was to just take the photos.

A little boy about five years old answered the door; I recognised him as the little boy that was to be returned to England. I asked the boy if his mother was at home.

But before the boy could answer a male voice said, "Can I help you?" I looked up and saw a young man in his mid 30's.

"Yes. Would Miss Donna please come as I have something for her," I said. Then before he could answer Miss Donna was standing at the front door as well.

"What do you want?" she said. "And who are you?

"My name is Rick. I am a process server from the court in England, and I have a court order for you madam," I replied.

Now that really upset the apple cart. I was walking a step backwards as I was speaking, so that Kai could get really good photos. Miss Donna immediately went inside the house and her boyfriend said that I should leave, that they would not accept any papers and that if I did not get off their property he would call the police.

I kept my cool and said, "You cannot refuse the documents sir; I will leave them here for you," and with that I put the papers on the path way and turned around in slow motion, so that Kai could get pictures of all the action.

As I left the front door slammed and the court orders just stayed where I had put them, on the front door step to the house.

I walked towards my car and was ready to drive off. I called Kai over to get in as we could now drive home — job finished. Kai got into the car and we sped off in the direction of home.

"Well Kai, did you get good pictures?" I said.

"Oh yes! I have taken at least twenty," he answered.

"Excellent," I said, and we drove off into the night.

After an hours or so driving I said, "Kai can you please drive for a while?" as I was really tired I had been driving non-stop since we left Cartagena City. I could not believe my ears when I heard Kai say, "I am sorry but I cannot drive as I do not have my glasses with me."

"What! Hey come on, Kai, I have to drive the whole three thousand kilometres?"

"Well, I am really sorry but I cannot see with out my glasses," Kai said.

For the next two hours not a word was spoken, just dead silence. I saw a motorway restaurant and so I pulled in so that we could have something to eat and get some coffee to keep me awake. I am sure that if I was traveling with someone and the driver had already driven 1,500 kilometres without a break, I would be shit scared! But that did not seem to worry ole Kai at all, he made a happy face and had some dinner and went back to sleep in the car. I felt sorry for Kai's wife as I realised how she had to put up with his snoring every night; but maybe she snored too and they had gotten used to it.

After a very well deserved break and half a litre of black coffee, I re-fuelled the car and drove back on the motorway at top speed. I drove all through the night. In retrospect, I think it was because I was so angry with Kai not bringing his glasses that kept me awake all the time, though the coffee helped too.

The black of the night turned back into the light of day and sunshine. Late in the afternoon, we arrived back in Cartagena, without incident or accident.

Kai and I did not speak much on the return trip, only what had to be said. I dropped Kai off at his house and went to my house. I telephoned the client and then the solicitors and said that I had completed the service and would get my report and photos off to them once I had some sleep.

I took all the bits and pieces from the car and put everything in my office with the all important camera. I needed sleep so badly that I did not even want a drink. I slept well and was at the same time happy that this was the best paid process service that I had ever undertaken and with a successful result. I really needed the cash.

I wrote my report and before going to the notary to swear an affidavit I took my film in to be developed in an Express One-Hour Photo Shop in the centre of town. The notary Margarita was on the ball and was not too busy so after 25 minutes I had my sworn affidavit. Now I needed to collect the photos as final evidence for the High Court in London. The shop owner and I had gotten to know each other quite well over the last year or so. When I walked into the photo shop in our town centre the lady shop assistant was giggling. I smiled and asked for my photos. Now the shop manageress was laughing and although my Spanish language was slowly getting better, I just did not know what the joke was about.

But then it became clear to me, the shop assistant put the envelope with the negatives and the photos — all 27 of them — in front of me.

Twenty seven big 24" by 27" colour glossy pictures — all of Kai's fingers. There was not really one picture we could use. I was livid. The shop assistant was thinking they were my fingers and was asking why I wanted so many pictures of my fingers!

"The price of cheap labour," I said, thinking that I had to pay for this crap as well. With my head bent in shame I returned to my office. Not one picture was usable for my report.

Kai had since returned to Sweden, luckily for him. In his eagerness to get the photos, Kai did not realise that his finger was in front of the lens. But fortunately for me, the target in Gerona had complained to the solicitors that I left his papers in the front garden, thus confirming that he had received the High Court orders. My client was happy with the process service.

I once again started to learn all about improving and updating my system, and investigated buying a digital camera.

After I had a couple of days off, which gave me time to read up and try and improve my services and I bought my first digital camera: a Casio EX P505 — the price: 750 Euros.

I was waiting for work to come in as usual. I liked my new profession more and more, with the excitement of a new case coming in every other day. Normally I would not even have a notion about other people's problems, now here I was helping to solve them.

When I saw the problems other people made for themselves it made me feel grateful that my problems were tiny in comparison.

21

Scams and Being Taken to the Cleaners

I receive about ten scams a day in my email inbox, (as I am sure many other people do too), even after my 'anti-scam' filter has done its best to filter out the scam messages.

You know it always surprises me how many people still fall for these scams, daily. I think it's the greed of people that the scammers play on, and they sometimes win.

Scams come in all varieties and often convey the cruelest messages to trick people. As I am sure you know, Nigeria is infamous for that very reason; but every day scammers are busy all over the world applying their trickery.

Mr. Parson, a Canadian gentleman telephoned me in the middle of the night asking me for some help. He explained that he had been informed that members of his family had been all killed in a horrific traffic accident in Barcelona two years ago. He had only just been informed about it. Mr. Parson wanted me to find out the names of his relatives that had been killed in December 2003. Mr. Parson said that they were from the German side of his family and that he had never met this side of his family in the past.

Why the sudden interest? sprang to my mind!

Mr. Parson was clearly a senior citizen, judging by the way he spoke and was very concerned about the whole affair. But when he asked what the enquiry would cost him he was shocked!

"Mr. Parson for me to go to Barcelona and back, get copies of the death certificates, and carry out a full investigation to confirm that all the people that had indeed been killed in the accident, would cost at least one thousand Euros or more," I told him.

Furthermore I informed Mr. Parson the reason that I would have to go to Barcelona in person to make the enquiries was because I would not be given any information over the telephone, because of the Data Protection Act, that had recently been introduced in Spain. I suggested that he could hire a private investigator in Barcelona and he snapped back at me, "Why can you not do the job?"

The phone was silent for about a minute.

"Hello, Mr. Parson, are you still there?" I asked.

"Yeah, I am still listening," he said.

"Mr. Parson, if I can find out from a newspaper or media report, then it will cost you a hundred and fifty Euros. But if I have to go to Barcelona to make the enquiries then it will cost a minimum of a thousand Euros, maybe more! If you want me to proceed then I would require a retainer of one thousand Euros paid by Western Union International Money Transfer," I said.

Mr. Parson was clearly agitated.

"Do you know how much money that is in Canadian dollars?" he yelled at me. "Sixteen hundred dollars. I work for a month for that kind of money!"

"OK, tell me where to send it," he reluctantly said.

I gave him the details for the Western Union office in my local town and I also asked him if he had access to a computer. He said that he didn't but his son did. He would send me the written instructions via his son and the money transfer numbers from the Western Union transfer.

I received the retainer and the written instructions the next day and I went to work. I telephoned Mr. Parson and confirmed that I had received the retainer and instructions. I asked Mr. Parson who had informed him of this accident, but he did not want to say.

The whole story smelt of scam so I contacted an agent in Barcelona to do some ground work for me while I was busy going through newspaper reports and the Internet; but it could not be confirmed that an accident had happened at all, as described by Mr. Parson.

I wrote another email to Mr. Parson saying that he had to tell me who informed him of the accident and why he was going to such great lengths to find out after two years about the people involved in the accident. I wondered why did Mr. Parson had not contacted his other relatives to find out. Things did not add up. Then at last he came clean with me.

Very reluctantly, Mr. Parson informed me that he was to inherit US $80 million that his German family had left to him. The solicitors and bank manager required his bank details and a $10,000 deposit from him to release the $80 million. I informed him that this must be a scam, but of course he did not want to believe it. He sent me a copy of the letter that the scammers had sent to him and I immediately saw two different Spanish bank logos on the letter heading on the same page of the scammer's letter requesting the $10,000.

I telephoned my client immediately.

"Mr. Parson please listen to me this is of grave importance! DO NOT give any bank details or any other personal details to these people! They are professional scammers and they will steal every penny that you have!"

The letter that he received was of course a fake. I gathered evidence from the Spanish banks concerned and with the evidence from the Barcelona agent and results of my enquiries, it was proven that this was just another scam.

I felt very sorry for Mr. Parson; I could just imagine him in his log cabin in the mountains of Canada covered in snow, feeling really disappointed, alone and stupid. He was of course not happy with the results but he also realised what could have happened if he had given his details and paid the release money of €1,000.

I telephoned Mr. Parson informing him that his bill had come to €1,250, and asked him to please send the balance of €250 to me via Western Union. I did not hear again from him for more than 3 weeks. I was going to send him a reminder to pay the balance but I didn't and thought about it. The poor man has been hurt enough so I decided to write him a letter. In my letter I explained that I was very sorry for the out come of the enquiry and that I accepted his €1,000 — in full and final settlement. I thanked him and wished him all the best for the future.

I was more than surprised to receive an email back from Mr. Parson' son in Canada, thanking me for helping his father from making one of the biggest mistakes of his life. His father apologised for the delay in settlement and sent me €500 — instead of the €250 that I had initially asked for. He said that I should keep the rest and take my lady out to dinner! What a gentleman, I thought. It was also the first time I had received a tip. God bless you Mr. Parson.

As the old saying goes: *If it sounds too good to be true then it most likely is not true.*

And a lot of poor people have had to find out the hard way.

Dearest Beloved, (or, Greetings to You From a Scammer)

First of all let me introduce myself to you; I am Sister Anita Adams Johnson from Ivory Coast. I am married to the late Chief Adams Johnson of blessed memory. My late husband was a produce merchant and contractor to the government on export of cacao. We were married for eleven years without a child, since his death I too have been battling with both cancer and fibroid problems.

Recently, I am in the hospital due to my critical health condition and my doctor told me that I would not last for few months and having known my condition I decided to donate my late husband's funds (US$ 8.7 million) deposited with a leading bank here to you so thatyou will utilize this money for yourself and also for the orphanages, widows and motherless organizations.

I will also issue an Order of authority to the bank, authorizing them that the said sum has been willed to you and a copy of such authorization will be forwarded to you. Any delay in your reply will give room in sourcing for another person / organization for this same purpose.

You may ask why I took this decision to transfer the fund to you. Why can't I withdraw from the fund to take care of my health???

Until I hear from you today unfailingly, I will give you detail information of the fundand get you cleared of these rhetorical questions.

Does it not make you feel sick? And there are hundreds more every day being emailed.

22

Confidence Tricksters at Work

There are con merchants all over the world and Spain is no exception, from small time crooks to the big time organised racketeering; we have the lot here in Spain. When I think of some of the cons I have seen in Spain, many of them are not even Spanish but the really bad offenders are the ex-pats — from all of Eastern Europe, Russians, British, Germans, French and Belgians. In fact the whole of the European Common Market is represented in scamming here, busily scamming each other.

A lot of the con artists can be found through the daily free newspapers and magazines found in any of the English shops, or any place like the community centers, where ex-pats may congregate in Spain. The bait is disguised in the free advertisements pages and they catch people every day.

A typical con is the really nice English builder that you telephoned from the free ads section and he says he guarantees all his work to English standards whatever they may be. (It must be said that the Spanish standards are very good today) And so you have called your newfound trusty builder, to take a look at fixing your plumbing or gas boiler that gave up on you, or the front gates to improve your security. He will tell you how he loves Spain and the better quality of life compared to wherever you may come from; he will congratulate you on making such a wise move to Spain; he will tell you about his kids going to school here and so on and that he knew people from your home town. But if he thinks you are anti-Spain and would prefer to be back in your own country he will then of course bad-mouth the Spanish. Either way he or she will dance to your tune.

He will also tell you about good jobs he has done in the past — that you have no way of finding out about — and you trust the man because he is so nice and he has 'Building Construction' written on his white Peugeot van parked in front of your house.

He knows when he has won your trust normally when you ask him if he would like a cup of tea. He gives you a quotation and asks for 50% up front to buy the materials and to be able to start with three men in the morning, so that your job will get the utmost attention and be finished in half the time that it would normally take! Once you have paid him the retainer, he will excuse himself saying that he has to get his men together for an early start for you in the morning. Then you never see the lying bastard again, if you are lucky, because more often than not if they start the job, they do not finish it as promised, and keep asking for more payments in cash from you.

If you do not see the builder again, you ring a week later to see if you can get your money back; but he is long gone. Serious and genuine workers are happy to be paid when the job is finished to your expectations and will give you a written quotation for the work that is to be carried out before they start, if you accept it.

There are con merchants absolutely everywhere out there waiting for you.

Here's another sample received by email daily.

```
Congratulations you have just won on the
European lottery and they want to pay you
millions...
```

but please give your bank details first and if you do so, instead of waking up a rich person you will wake up a very, very poor person!

RICK HOWATSON

FROM REV. DENISE DEAN
MENARA MANULIFE RB,
6 JALAN GELENGGANG,
DAMANSARA HEIGHTS,
50490 KUALA LUMPUR,
MALAYSIA, 56000

GOOD DAY

I COME TO YOU WITH LOVE AND GRATITUDE TO
GOD FOR OUR LIVES AND THE OPPORTUNITIES
GRANTED UNTO US TO BE CONNECTED TODAY FOR
A BENEFICIAL BUSINESS THAT WILL LAST FROM
GENERATION TO GENERATION IF ONLY YOU WILL
GIVE ME YOUR SUPPORT. MEANWHILE PERMIT ME TO
INTRODUCE MYSELF BELOW.

I AM REV. DANISE DEAN, OF HSBC BANK PLC
(H.B.) I AM WRITING IN RESPECT OF A FOREIGN
CUSTOMER OF MY BANK LATE ENGR. CHRISTIAN
EICH (SNR) A NATIONAL OF YOUR COUNTRY, WHO
USED TO WORK WITH SHELL DEVELOPMENT COMPANY
HERE IN MALAYSIA.
ON MONDAY 31 JULY 2000. HIS WIFE AND TWO
OF HIS CHILDREN WERE INVOLVED IN AIRCRAFT
CRASH. ALL OCCUPANTS UNFORTUNATELY LOST
THEIR LIVES.
FOR MORE INFOMATION VISIT THE WEB SITE :
http://news.bbc.co.uk/1/hi/world/
europe/859479.stm

SINCE THEN BANK AND I HAVE MADE SEVERAL
ENQUIRIES TO YOUR EMBASSY TO LOCATE ANY OF
HIS IMMEDIATE RELATIVES THIS HAS ALSO PROVED
ABORTIVE. AFTER THESE SEVERAL UNSUCCESSFUL
ATTEMPTS I HAVE CONTACTED YOU TO ASSIST
IN CLAIMING THE MONEY AND PROPERTIES LEFT
BEHIND BY OUR CUSTOMER BEFORE THEY GET
CONFISCATED OR DECLARED UNSERVICEABLE BY
OUR BANK WHERE HE DEPOSITED THE SUM OF
SEVENTEEN MILLION, FIVE HUNDRED THOUSAND
UNITED STATES DOLLARS.
  SINCE IT IS THE LAW SAY THAT IF THE FUNDS
ARE UNCLAIMED AT THE EXPIRATION OF 10 YEARS
THE FUNDS WILL BE DIVERT THE HER MAJESTY'S
ACCOUNT.
  I GUARANTEE YOU THAT THIS TRANSACTION WILL
BE EXECUTED UNDER LEGITIMATE ARRANGEMENT
THAT WILL PROTECT YOU AND I FROM ANY BREACH
OF THE LAW. DO CALL ME NOW +01673231920
  UPON THE RECEIPT OF YOUR RESPONSE I WILL
DETAIL YOU ON THE MODALITIES THROUGH WHICH
WE WILL ACHIEVE THIS CLAIMS. HOPING TO HEAR
FROM YOU SOON, REMAIN BLESSED, CALL ME NOW
IF YOU ARE INTRESTED.

MY REGARDS,
REV. DANISE DEAN
ACCOUNT MANAGER
HSBC BANK PLC (O.B)
PRIVATE NUMBER +01673231920

If it sounds too good to be true, then it usually is!

23

The Stone-crusher Con

A 50-tonne stone crushing machine does not sound very interesting does it; or that someone could scam millions with it? Well does it? Put a price tag of 350,000 Euros per machine, find you have been conned out of 6 machines and that your competition is in the process of buying the same machines that you had bought and paid for but not had delivered; then it becomes very interesting.

Figure 1 One stone-crusher—we were looking for three of them!

One Down; Two More to Find

I received a call from Dick Miller, an Englishman working for a large gravel company in the USA. "We need your help, buddy," he said and he proceeded to tell me some of the story, asking if I would be available at once to carry out the investigation to find his missing machines. Dick said he did not care what it cost his company as long as I got the required results and that was to find three 50-tonne stone crushing machines! Surely no one can hide a 50-tonne machine I thought; but I was wrong; they can and they did.

The gravel company that Dick worked for in America had ordered and paid for six stone crushing machines, over two million Euros, to a specialist stone crushing sales company registered in Austria.

The same company was represented in the USA as well as in Spain and other countries by means of the Internet, but they were to be proved fake companies. The con trick that they used was to show and sell the same machine as many times as they possibly could, changing the serial numbers after the machine had been shown and then moved on to be hidden in another quarry high up in the mountains of Granada.

After the ordered stone crushing machines delivery failed to happen in the USA, the gravel company sent Dick over to Spain to try and find out just what was going on after hearing too many excuses from the directors of the Austrian company, Dick travelled to Spain and arranged to meet the people that stated that the machines were actually in Spain and just waiting to be delivered to the USA.

Dick arrived and was met by an Austrian lady called Stefanie von Schmoll; she spoke German, Spanish and English fluently. It was Stefanie's brother that was the managing director of the Austrian company. She collected Dick from Malaga International Airport and took him to a very nice 5-star hotel in Benalmadena on the coast near Malaga. She drove the latest Mercedes 500 C class, champagne colour. Dick was wined and dined by Stefanie and then the next morning she arranged to meet Dick and take him to the quarry site up in the mountains, where the stone crushing machines were, and supposedly waiting to be shipped to America.

The next morning Stefanie collected Dick as arranged and everything looked good so far. Stefanie drove Dick to a quarry where there was a new 50-tonne stone-crusher. Dick checked the serial numbers and yes it was most certainly the very same one that belonged to his company.

A low-loader is a very special heavy duty lorry and trailer that specialises in transporting big machines and would normally have to be cleared by the traffic police to travel on the public roads, and have an escort vehicle with flashing lights. In the quarry was a low-loader that was waiting for the stone-crusher to be loaded, with instructions to take it to the Port of Malaga for immediate shipping to America. So far Dick was pleased with his initial the results of his trip.

Stefanie had wined and dined Dick well and I am sure if he wanted she would have slept with him at no extra cost. Dick still quite rightly did not trust Stefanie and what was about to happen. The plan was that the low-loader was to collect the stone-crusher and deliver it to the port of Malaga for shipping to the USA. Dick was to say thank you very much now, let us look for the other machines But Dick did not want to let the stone-crusher out of eye sight so he demanded Stefanie drive behind the low-loader and with him escort the big machine to the port.

The stone-crusher was loaded on to the low-loader and without a police escort drove off on to the public highway. After two hours of driving the low-loader pulled into a fuelling station and stopped. Stefanie explained that the driver by law must have a rest before he could continue his journey. Dick and Stefanie went into the gas station café for coffee.

Stefanie then said that the driver had problems with the Spanish customs and port authorities and that she needed 85,000 Euros to clear the machine. Dick said that was it not in the contract that clearance money had to be paid and you do not pay customs on goods leaving a country, only when they come in to the country and no way would his company be paying any more money to Stefanie.

Dick finished his coffee and Stefanie said she had to go to the ladies room and so Dick waited and waited for her to return; but she did not return. When Dick left the restaurant and walked out onto the parking bays there was no low-loader and no Mercedes, and Dick was not even sure of where the hell he was. By the time Dick had realised what had happened, Stefanie and the low-loader were long gone. Dick ordered a taxi and drove 180 miles back to his 5-star hotel in Malaga only to find out that Stefanie had checked out of the hotel and left him to pay all the hotel bills.

Dick returned back to the USA very pissed off, and telephoned me.

Dick had a new lead; an American colleague named Stephen Goodman that was in the same gravel trade business in the USA and would normally be his competitor. However, not only had Stephen heard that Dick's company had been duped, but Stephen had also spoken to the same Jochen von Schmoll, the director of the Austrian company, as a potential customer. He was told that the Austrian company had just acquired the machines that he wanted to buy — at a special discounted rate. The potential buyer would have to pay a $50,000 deposit retainer and then fly to Spain to inspect the machines.

The two American gravel companies decided to work together and help each other. Stephen agreed to fly to Spain with his wife and child and Dick's company agreed to pay the $50,000 deposit if Stephen would be the undercover man working with me, to lead us to the stone crushing machines.

You may remember I said earlier in the book that everyone is a contact, and you may also remember the story about Tom Hyland's construction company in Ireland. I gave Tom a call about these stone crushing machines and he was delighted to hear from me and I was delighted to hear from him. Lucky for me Tom was an expert on stone crushing machines; so he was now not only my technical back-up but he was also ready to fly over from Ireland to Spain if I needed a driver for the machines. Tom proved to be a great help.

Stephen and his little family arrived as planned in Spain and were met at Malaga International Airport by Stefanie; only this time she was not alone! Inga and I were already at the airport waiting to follow Stefanie's every move, and Stephen and his family. The plane was late but that is usual. At 4:00 p.m. Stephen came out of the airport with his wife, son and Stefanie.

Stefanie packed the family and their travel bags in her new champagne coloured Mercedes and drove off in the direction of Benamaldina, just 25 miles from the airport. Stefanie stopped outside the beautiful 5-star hotel, where she had two rooms booked, for herself and Stephen's family.

Inga and I waited for two hours to see if Stefanie would come out of the hotel and possibly stay somewhere else, but she didn't. I received a call from Dick in the USA, confirming that Stephen had called him confirming that Stefanie had booked all of them into the hotel and would be staying there that night and leaving at 10:00 a.m. the next morning, to have a look at a stone crushing machine that was for sale.

I checked into the hotel and requested back-up from two of our agents in Marbella, to assist with the surveillance and tailing the Mercedes in the morning as I knew there would be a lot of traffic on the roads and to follow the Mercedes could prove very difficult. Later in the evening we saw Stephen, his wife, son and Stefanie going for dinner in the hotel restaurant and then after dinner they talked for an hour or so before they both retired and went to their respective hotel rooms.

The next morning at 10:00 our agents were on time, but I was not. Julio, one of our agents telephoned me and confirmed that he was in the hotel car park waiting for action and ready to follow the targets. But I was not the only person to oversleep, so did Inga, and so did Stefanie and Stephen and his family.

At 12:00 midday finally Stefanie and Stephen finally came out of the hotel with Stephen's wife and seven-year-old boy.

Stefanie drove from the car park to the entrance of the hotel and Stephen and his family got into the car and drove off in the direction of Malaga. Julio was hot behind them and followed them for about 100 miles. Stefanie then left the motorway and into a small town called Nerja. Everybody got out of Stefanie's Mercedes and went into a small café. Julio had driven past the café and then stopped and turned back, only to see Stefanie come out of the café with Stephen and family and drive off in the Mercedes again, in the direction of Granada. Julio was now on the wrong side of the road to follow; he had a long way to go before he could turn around to catch up and follow the Mercedes again. I was now in front of the Mercedes so I slowed down and it eventually overtook my car. We took some good close-up photos of Stefanie as she was overtaking us.

I received a call from Dick in the USA. We had a problem; Stefanie told Stephen that she was scared and that she was sure she was being followed and that is why she had to stop in Nerja to make some telephone calls; the result being that she had taken the registration number of Julio's car and she now had people following his car. This was really getting to be a cat and mouse game.

I telephoned Julio and told him to abort and return to Marbella; give the car that was following him a good run for their money and then change vehicles. We have five cars and a motorcycle for quick changes already prepared for this job.

Julio really enjoyed the game and we were still tailing behind Stefanie's champagne Mercedes but she had not noticed us.

Stefanie drove through Granada and another 200 miles north to the town of Almeria; it was getting quite late. She stopped at a small roadhouse hotel for the night. We had the pleasure of sleeping in the car waiting for the next move on surveillance, but no stone crushing machines had been seen that day!

Dick called me again from the USA informing us that Stephen was again warning us to be very careful. Stefanie had said that Spain was a very dangerous country if you drove an upmarket car like hers. She believed she was being followed, so she had requested security from her brother's company to follow the car that she thought was tailing her. The truth was that Julio had changed cars back in Marbella and driven home and was fast asleep in his bed by this time; though Stefanie's men were reporting that they were still following Julio's car! Stephen had also said that Stefanie was taking him to see the stone-crusher in the morning.

10 am — The next morning we had just finished the cold coffee that we had left in the flask when out came Stefanie and Stephen with his family without any warning! They all got into the Mercedes and drove back in the direction of Malaga. We kept our distance. Stefanie had more confidence now that she was not being followed, but she was driving in circles and now drove 250 miles south to the beautiful Spanish city of Granada.

Once in Granada Stefanie drove 30 miles to a small mountain village called Durcal. Inga and I saw many quarry signs and knew that we must be quite close to the stone-crusher.

Obviously Stephen had no idea that he was being driven around in circles to confuse him. He really did not have a clue where he was now.

When Stefanie arrived at the quarry site, I pulled off the road just past the quarry and waited. The track leading up the mountain into the quarry was very small with many bends in and I did not want to blow my cover by driving up to the quarry! And with the possibility of meeting Stefanie on the way down again. It was better that I stay put until Julio arrived. I telephoned Julio to come to Granada and I explained exactly where we were. Two hours later Julio arrived and joined us. We had a chat about what was going on. As we were speaking, Stefanie's Mercedes came back down the mountain track with her guests and back onto the main road leading back to Granada city. Our big question was: Is the bloody stone-crusher up there in the quarry or not?!

I had to know, so I sent Julio to tail Stefanie while Inga and I drove up the mountain track and after what seemed like half an eternity of six miles along a very bad track, on our left we saw the huge yellow stone-crusher. Whoopee and hallelujah; it was really there! We did not stop but carried on up the mountain as if we were lost tourists and turned around. On the way down again Inga got some fantastic photos of the machine and we drove on back down to the main road again.

I telephoned Dick back in the States to update him on the situation; he was delighted. "Now stay with that machine and do not leave it, and should it move, then follow it," came the instructions from Dick. In the meantime Julio had called back to say that he was on his way back to Almeria. I told Julio the news about the stone-crusher and that we would have to take shifts in guarding the machine when he returned. I called in more support from Marbella and two more agents were on their way to meet me and stay the night. Now I needed to get back to my office, 400 miles south of Granada, to get some tracking devices to be able to track the machine if it was being moved.

A tracking device is an accurate, battery-operated device that sends a signal, which is bounced back from a satellite in the atmosphere to a computer monitor that picks up the signal and can give its exact location. Once the tracker has been fixed onto any vehicle or machine with a clear view of the sky, all movements can be monitored.

When the agents arrived from Malaga, I updated them on the scenario. They informed us that they were armed with handguns, as in the mountains the security guards are always armed at night in the quarries. I thought that rather strange but when it was explained to me that there is not only were there very expensive machines to be had in the quarries, but also explosives and there had been break-ins in the past by terrorist organisations, it now made complete sense to me why the quarries are so heavily guarded. I was thinking of getting my toy gun, but then common sense prevailed and it was staying at home.

Inga and I arrived back in Cartagena City around midnight to sort the tracking devices out and to get some well earned sleep. That night Julio had to sleep in his car outside the same roadhouse hotel in Almeria as we had previously; our two agents from Malaga were on guard duty in the village of Durcal guarding the stone-crusher.

The agents had been up the mountain and established that if the stone-crusher was to be moved it could only come one way; that was down the mountain. The road leading up the mountain finished after 12 miles, at a dead end. To move the machine would require a large low-loader to carry it anywhere, which would be seen going up. So we were confident that we had the stone-crusher in check mate; but where were the other machines?

Back in my office in Cartagena, I established that the Mercedes that Stefanie was so proudly driving around was of course a hired car.

Midday — armed with two tracking devices we returned to the village of Durcal, to take over from the night shift. After the two agents reported the current situation and that all was well, I sent the agents for some rest in a nearby hostel. We were working 12-hour shifts now.

"Inga if we could get the tracking devices on the machine then we could take things easier, but the stone-crusher is the centre of attraction and well guarded," I said. I have mentioned before that Inga has always shown a lot of courage, considering her young age, and she immediately volunteered to place the trackers on the machine.

Now this was really a risky move and I was not prepared to risk our necks and especially the beautiful neck of Inga just so that we could keep track of the stone-crusher, so I said we would wait until we had the opportune moment and then strike to place the tracker on the stone-crusher machine.

We did however drive back up to the stone-crusher before the security guards came on duty and Inga took some close-up pictures of the serial numbers of the machine.

I was receiving results now from the company searches that I had initiated back in Cartagena; the Austrian company had been declared bankrupt, and that was 12 months earlier. The addresses we had for Stefanie and her brother did not prove to be correct and all the different business cards for Stefanie and her brother we had been sent copies of from the USA were fakes, but very good fakes just the same.

The big concern now was that Stefanie would come and move the machine under our noses, and legally we could do nothing to stop her. If push came to shove it would have been her word against our word, and Stefanie would be off in a flash with the stone-crusher.

I asked Dick if we could go to the local police and ask for assistance but he did not want to get them involved as they were far too slow to act and we had no real evidence to prove what she was up to.

The serial numbers that we had taken photographs of were identical to the invoiced machine that Dick had purchased from the Austrian company, and also the machine that our undercover man Stephen had been shown the day before to purchase.

In the meantime I received a panic call from Dick; he needed me to return to the 5-star hotel in Malaga and get into Stephen's room and take a hidden mobile telephone out of his laptop bag. Stephen was now getting really scared — he had telephone numbers of Dick and the agents on his telephone and was very worried that if one of Stefanie's henchmen found it they would know that he was working undercover.

I waited for the day shift to return and then drove to the 5-star hotel in Malaga but I was uneasy about trying to get into a guest room as I was no longer booked into the hotel. The presence of security guards was clearly everywhere.

Inga and I walked into the reception, said "hello" with a friendly wave to the staff on the reception desk and then headed up to the seventh floor to Stephen's room, as if we were guests of the hotel. I could not see any CCTV in the hallways but that did not mean to say that they did not have them. Inga and I boldly went to Stephen's door and with our old card key card tried to open the door, but of course it did not work. So I called one of the chamber maids and asked if she would kindly assist as I had problems with my key card.

"Not a problem" she said and promptly opened the door for us. "Thank you so much," I said and we quickly went inside the room. We searched everywhere and eventually we found the laptop but could not find the mobile telephone. I did not want to stay in the room longer than necessary in case a CCTV had picked us up, so after five minutes we left the room and I thanked the cleaning lady again as we walked off towards the lifts.

Once we were on the ground level I telephoned Dick.

"Dick we could not find the mobile telephone," I said. Dick waited a moment and then said he would call me back as he needed to call Stephen and ask him exactly where he had hidden the mobile phone; maybe the bad guys had already found it!

Stephen was now somewhere in the region of Almeria.

Twenty minutes later Dick called me back.

"Stephen has his telephone hidden in a secret compartment in the laptop bag."

"Thanks Dick," I said.

So Inga and I went back into the hotel again and made our way up to the 7th floor and tried the same trick and it worked; the chamber maid opened the door again. I said that I would go back down to the reception and change my key card and gave the chamber maid 10 Euros for her help and she was very happy. Inga and I quickly opened the laptop bag, found where the telephone was hidden and took it out and then left the room and returned to the car. I called Dick and told him we had the telephone and he was satisfied that Stephen was no longer in danger of being found out.

I telephoned Julio to find out if he was still tailing Stefanie's Mercedes, and he was. They were all still in Almeria.

Bit by bit, the pieces of this weird jigsaw puzzle were coming together.

To summarise:
- The Austrian company that sold the stone crushing machines was bankrupt and had been for over a year.
- The detail we had been given about the two directors being Jochen and his sister Stefanie was fabricated.
- We could not locate any assets so it did not look good for the American gravel company of ever getting their money back, unless we could find out where all the machines were.
- We had located one stone crushing machine for Dick in Durcal Quarry that was now being guarded.
- We were tailing Stefanie and our undercover man, hoping to locate more machines. Inga and I were on our way to Durcal Quarry to place the tracker on to the machine, so that if the machine was moved we can track its movements.
- With six agents and three cars all working on the case at this point in time, we were doing our utmost for a successful outcome.

Stephen and his family had certainly been given the runaround by Stefanie but I could not see what Stefanie was trying to prove by driving around for so many miles. Stephen was still booked in at the 5-star hotel in Malaga and the hotel tab was still running but she was actually staying in a two-bit roadhouse hotel in Almeria.

Stephen now for the first time telephoned me directly and said that in the morning Stefanie wanted to take him to see some more machines in a town called Cata something or other.

"Stephen, I need you please to be more precise," I said. "Well I will call you back when I know more," he replied and hung up on me.

I needed to find the other machines. The two support agents from Malaga had come to take over for the night shift at the quarry in Durcal. Inga and I were really glad to leave; our observation point was by a collection of garbage bins that stank really badly in the day time when we had temperatures of 35 degrees plus. Not even the rats came out to play here; this they did at night.

As the agents took up position I thought it was now or never so Inga and I drove up the mountain track to where the stone crushing machine was.

As soon as we saw it Inga jumped out of the car and like a little monkey climbed up onto the engine platform and placed a tracker behind the engine cover and within seconds she was back in the car. I really admired her courage and agility. The tracker was the size of a third of a shoe box, black in colour and giving off a little red signal to the satellite above it. The tracker must have a clear view to be able to send a signal to the satellite; then the satellite sends the signal back to us so that we can track its position. The tracker has a battery life of four weeks but then it has to be recharged; it also has the ability to shift into 'sleep' mode and re-activate itself when the tracker is moving.

We drove down the mountain and informed our agents that we had placed the tracker, and warned them to watch out for any low-loader that might suddenly appear and drive up the mountain.

Inga and I needed something to eat so we drove into Granada City to a McDonald's. I personally do not like McDonald's but Inga loves it and I thought she deserved it after placing the tracker.

We received reports that the tracker was working well, sending signals back to London to the agents that were monitoring the tracker. We could follow now it with Google Earth if the machine was to be moved.

After a Big Mac and chips we walked back to the car. This time on arrival I received a call directly from Stephen again.

"Hey, Stefanie has told me that we are travelling to a town two hundred fifty miles south of here, called Cata-something."

"Cartagena," I filled in for him.

"Hey that's it; that's where we are going in the morning," said Stephen.

"Good work Stephen. And is Stefanie still chasing that car in Marbella?" I asked.

"Well she just said that security took care of it, period," answered Stephen.

Now it was time to leave the stone-crusher machine and drive home and on the way change places with Julio so he could return to Durcal and take over the next day shift, guarding the stone-crusher. I could follow Stefanie, Stephen and family to Cartagena.

In the early hours of the morning we met Julio and his companion in Almeria in the car park opposite the hotel where Stefanie was staying and told him that we would take over the surveillance and Julio was to return to Durcal.

Julio is a very likeable person and very reliable and just a pleasure to work with. It is so important that you have good company when you have to sit in a car for hours in the cold of the night, (that turns into an oven during the day,) just waiting for something to happen.

Things were now all on site, and Julio was very pleased to be able to change location. I told him about the tracker being on the machine; this made life for everyone much easier. It would not be too long before Julio would be able to return to his lovely Irish wife in Marbella.

Stefanie was up bright and early with her potential clients and on the motorway by 10:30. From Almeria we travelled back to Cartagena City. The Mercedes was an easy car to follow from a distance because of its unusual champagne colour. We followed without incident until we were just 15 miles from Cartagena. Stefanie had left the motorway and disappeared! We did not see her go! We were so near, yet so far away.

I telephoned Dick in the States and asked him to call Stephen, to give us some clues as to where they might be! Stephen called me and before I answered, he immediately started speaking.

"Well hi Mom, we are having a wonderful time here in Spain. Right now we can see the sailing boats in the harbour and we are having a nice meal in a restaurant on the water front. Well, bye Mom," he finished, and hung up.

Now we knew exactly where he was and we drove straight to the port of Cartagena. We parked the car and walked on the promenade of the yacht marina, looking at the millions of dollars in boats moored there — truly a wonderful sight. For the first time we saw Stephen and his family with Susan, drinking coffee. I was wondering what lies she was telling him at that moment.

It was a really good feeling to know that we had the subjects back in sight and under our control again. We went back to the car and waited for Stefanie's next move and we did not have long to wait.

Stefanie left the harbour restaurant with her guests and walked over to the underground car park. She drove out of the underground car park just as I had expected and we slowly followed in pursuit. Stefanie was clearly showing the sights to her clients and stopped a few times to explain this or that.

Cartagena is a wonderful city to explore, with evidence of its Roman origins everywhere and the presence of warships in the harbor was evident that Cartagena is the home of the Spanish Royal Navy, and its headquarters.

Stefanie drove only three miles out of Cartagena and then sharp left into a quarry that we never even knew existed. We drove on past and stopped a mile down the road at a pullover area. I telephoned Dick in the USA.

"Dick I think we may have found some more stone-crushers."

At the same moment a security jeep pulled up next to me; I saw that the man was armed and my eyes were fixed on his hand gun. The security guard asked me what I was doing there.

"Can you not see I am telephoning?" I answered. He looked a bit confused.

"Well," he said, "the lady in the Mercedes that drove into the quarry just now said that you were following her."

"What lady? What Mercedes? I do not know what you are talking about," I replied.

"Oh, then I am sorry to have troubled you sir," he answered and left.

I waited till the security guard was out of sight and then we drove past the quarry entrance; Inga was busy taking photographs of the quarry entrance as we drove past.

"That was it," I said. "Now we need to go home and change cars." My home was only a 25-minute drive away but I drove it in 15 minutes.

Once we arrived back in the office I checked the GPS location of the stone-crusher in Durcal near Granada and it was still in position and had not been moved. I telephoned Julio who was enjoying himself at home and asked him if he would take the next day shift and to relieve the other two agents and send them home and to take over from the other two agents in Durcal guarding the machine, and that I would take over the next shift from him then in the morning. Julio was pleased to get the work as surveillance is well paid so he agreed, which gave me time to go back to the quarry in Cartagena to see if there were any more stone-crushers there.

I drove back on my own. Next to the very heavily guarded quarry was an old road that once led to a dormant Guardia Civil police barracks. As I drove up this road I was surprised to see that the whole quarry was wire fenced, along with security guards.

I drove into the pound of the old Guardia barracks that was now nothing more than a shell of a building in ruins. I walked around and climbed up the stairway onto the roof; there I had a splendid view of at least six stone crushing machines. Yippee, I had found them! I quickly took about 20 photos of the quarry with its machines and then decided very quickly to get off government owned land — I did not want to be arrested for trespassing now!

Back in the car I drove home and called Dick in the USA again and he was delighted with the news. But there was no way that we could enter the quarry to put a tracking device on the machines; well not yet anyway.

I drove home and had some sleep before getting ready to return to Durcal again. Everything was going to plan and we had nearly completed our assignment. But there was trouble ahead still to come...

Con men and women are like snakes in a trap when they realise that the game is nearly up; with confidence they fight to the bitter end before disappearing into the smoke clouds of modern

Europe only to re-appear somewhere else in different clothes, different names and with a different con. They will carry on in the con profession until they retire on a sunny beach in the Bahamas or some where equally as nice on their ill gotten money, or end up rotting away in a prison cell; or maybe some of them become politicians — oooops, sorry!

Inga called: she was ready to be collected to go back down to Granada with me to relieve Julio and his colleague. We left early and arrived at midday, though I did not see any great need anymore; we knew where the machines were and we had a tracker on the machines if they were to be moved from Durcal. However our instructions were very clear: stay on the job until we received other instructions from Dick in the USA.

We met up with Julio and I invited him and his colleague to lunch in a bar opposite the quarry. After lunch Julio told me that he had seen a lot of Guardia Civil cars going up to the quarry so there must have been some trouble up there. The guards were very heavily armed in what looked like riot gear.

Julio wanted to find out what was going on; so as we took up our observation point positions by the smelly garbage bins, Julio drove up alone to where the stone-crusher was. Ten minutes later my car-phone was ringing and I picked up. Julio was talking, not directly to me but to some one else, sending me a coded message.

"Help, I have been arrested and being taken to police head quarters in Durcal," I heard him say, and then the line went dead.

We all looked on as we saw Julio in one of the three police cars coming down the track. So we did what we do best and followed them.

I drove to Durcal village centre and found where the police station was and sure enough Julio was being led in handcuffs into the police station. Inga and I got out of the car and went to the information desk at the police station; but before we could say anything a policeman told us to sit down and wait as they were very busy. After a few minutes I called the guard over and said I needed to speak to his senior officer. Then just as he was about to tell me to sit down again, I pulled my badge and ID out. He was really impressed.

"Yes sir! Please, I will tell him at once," he said, in response to my request.

A minute later the door opened and I could see poor old Julio sitting down on a wooden chair looking at me as if to say, "Help me!" I walked into the office saying hello to Julio and again I waved my Spanish detective badge and ID at the officer. The police officer was very kind and asked Inga and I to sit down.

I could see the sigh of relief in Julio's face as he noticed the tone of the music had now changed from hostile to friendly.

"Julio is one of my men," I said, to the officer. Julio's handcuffs were immediately removed and the officer asked me to explain what was going on.

I told him that we were all working undercover, to expose a worldwide con that was being carried out on Spanish territory by foreign nationals, not Spanish nationals, and that we were collecting evidence before we were brought charges against the perpetrators.

The officer told me that Stefanie and Stephen had visited the machine last night and someone had noticed a red flashing signal on the stone-crusher, and said it must be a bomb. The Spanish equivalent of the S.W.A.T. team and the anti-bomb unit had been called in and the area cleared. At first, if they could not identify the device they were going to blow the machine up. Now that would not have pleased the Americans to have their beloved stone-crusher blown up because of our tracking device! A tracking device would cost me £750 if I lost it as well!

The door to the office opened and another officer came into the room, looked at me and smiled.

"I suppose this belongs to you," he said and handed over my tracking device.

"Thank you very much, sir," I said.

I explained to the guards what was going on with the stone-crusher and we came to the conclusion that charges should be made against Stefanie, otherwise there was nothing that the police could do to help us. If we tried to stop Stefanie from taking the machine then we would be violating the law, and they would have to assist Stefanie.

At this point I called Dick in the USA again and explained that the police would take over guarding the machine but only if an emergency impounding order could be made, stopping Stefanie from removing the machine. Dick knew it made sense what I was saying and he contacted the American Embassy in Malaga to employ a criminal lawyer to file charges on his behalf against Stefanie and her devious brother Jochen.

Julio, Inga and I left the police station and Julio drove straight home to Malaga; he had had enough excitement for one day.

Inga and I stayed in Durcal, guarding the machines.

The lawyer that was employed by Dick called me for an emergency meeting. I insisted that we had to meet on site as the stone-crusher could still legally be collected and taken away at any moment.

The lawyer, Alex was his name, was a good man and he came down late afternoon around 7:00 p.m. We showed him the stone-crusher, serial numbers and the evidence that we had gathered. Alex was just as impressed with us as we were with him and so that was a great foundation to work from.

Alex, our lawyer and I visited the police station and he filed charges against Stefanie and her brother and requested an emergency impounding order until the court would decide who the machine belonged to. In the meantime we had to wait by the garbage bins until further notice; the other support agents had now returned to Marbella; that left only Julio, Inga and me.

Julio returned the next day and took the first shift again and Inga and I went to the hostel to get some sleep and food. The next morning we had heard nothing from the lawyers about the impounding orders.

I met Julio at the observation point. Locals were walking past us now and greeting us, saying "good morning" to us as if we were a natural part of the landscape. Julio and I went to the workers' bar and had morning coffee with some of the workers from the quarry and then Julio left for the hostel to get some sleep.

Julio had made friends with the owner of the quarry and found out a few things: the machine was for sale; it was now being offered at a discounted half price. He had bought a stone crushing machine from Stefanie for half price himself and in the agreement he committed himself to allow Stefanie and her brother to park and display other machines on his quarry land from time to time, with the purpose of selling them.

At 11:30 a.m. things were happening again. A huge low-loader was very slowly making its way up the track of the mountain, and in front was a small Peugeot car with Stefanie driving with a male passenger; of course we followed.

At the same time I called the lawyer Alex, informing him of what was happening.

"Keep them there. I am on my way," he instructed.

I telephoned Julio and asked him to call the quarry owner and that he would also be charged for assisting an offender, if he didn't help stall whatever Stefanie had planned.

It took half an hour for the low-loader to drive up the mountain and into the quarry parking area. Stefanie and her male friend went to look at the stone-crusher. Inga was busy taking photographs and I went over to the driver of the low-loader and asked him if he was a private contractor or if we could hire him. He said that he was not available today but I could telephone his office; he gave me his business card and said that he would be happy to work for me if I had a job for him to do. I asked if he needed a police escort to transport the stone-crusher and he said yes; Stefanie his client was responsible for arranging it.

I telephoned the police chief in Durcal explaining that Stefanie was here to collect the machine.

"There is nothing we can do!" the police chief said.

"I think you can," I said. "Has there been an application made to the traffic police for an escort for the low-loader?"

"Not that we know of," was his reply.

"So it would be illegal to drive on a public motorway without an escort; is that correct?" I said.

"OK, we will check it out," he agreed.

"Thank you so much," I said.

Stefanie now returned with a middle aged Spanish gentleman who was her passenger and spoke to the driver of the low-loader. Just at that moment the cavalry arrived: Alex, our lawyer. He drove over to me for a quick update and then we both went over and had a talk with the quarry owner. Stefanie's male passenger, we then discovered, was the new purchaser of the stone-crusher. Stefanie looked at me with her evil eyes and she knew that she had seen me before but could not quite remember where!

Alex said that Stefanie could not remove the machine as it did not belong to her.

"The machine had just been sold to the gentleman standing by my side," Stefanie triumphantly declared. (According to my calculation, this particular machine had now been sold four times in four days.)

The quarry owner did not want to get involved so he backed off. Alex said that the case was up for a special hearing in the Granada Courts in the morning and that Stefanie and her brother had to attend. Stefanie started to show her real nasty unladylike face and started to shout at Alex, but Alex took no notice.

The police arrived and asked the driver of the low-loader if he had requested an escort? The driver said that Stefanie had made a request; but then it materialised that Stefanie had *not* made a request. Such a request takes three days to process and he would not be allowed to move the low-loader without being cleared by the traffic police. Alex looked at me and said, "Well done! You should become a lawyer."

Stefanie left with her client in a really bad mood and a cloud of dust in her little humble eight-year-old Peugeot; quite a come down from the Mercedes.

Alex, Inga and I went to the hostel where Julio was staying and had a fantastic dinner to celebrate our winning the day. Stefanie was not to be trusted and may still have something up her sleeve, so we had to remain vigilant on guard by the garbage bins at the foot of the mountain until we received new instructions.

Dick was happy with events and said we could stand down once the impounding order was in place. In the meantime more machines had been located in America that had been sold as many as eight times to different buyers; these machines also had impounding orders on them. Interpol, with the Austrian police, had found a machine for printing engine serial numbers on metal plaques and this was major evidence of how the swindlers had worked their con and could get away with it.

The next day Alex confirmed that the impounding order was now in place and that I would be required at a later stage to give evidence in the criminal courts in Granada. Needless to say, neither Stefanie nor her brother turned up to appear for court, nor were they represented.

I saw the driver of the low-loader walking down the mountain track, as we were leaving our observation point. I drove over to him and I asked if he was OK.

He said, "Yes. I am on my way to the police to have that bitch Stefanie charged, as she went off without paying me!"

We gave him a lift to the police station and then hit the road for home — job done!

Figure 2 Stone-crusher, now impounded by the police.

24

Authorities Clamp Down on Foreign Investigators in Spain

I have now been in business for several years in Spain and I am very happy with the way things have gone in general; I am not rich, but satisfied. There is something new always lurking around the corner.

I have become a well known face at the European conferences over the years and I have always tried my best to keep up-to-date with things, but for some time now, especially in Catalonia in the north of Spain, the Spanish private investigators are very unhappy and have complained continually about foreigner investigators working in Spain, on their turf, stealing their work; and not being as qualified as they are — which is a fair comment.

You see the Spanish private investigators must have a 5-year university education that ends up with a Bachelor of Arts and a Masters degree in law. Foreigners coming into Spain have in the past since the European Common Market, not needed any special requirements or license to work in Spain; but as of November 7th 2007, they now do.

The Spanish government was lobbied by the Spanish private investigators and Private Detectives Trade Associations and its membership to have legislation passed to make it illegal for people from other European member states to work in Spain without an appropriate license, issued from the Ministry of the Interior. The pre-requisite for a Spanish license is that you must have the same law degree as the Spanish do, and that you must also speak fluent Spanish. That's a bit hard on us old foreign fellows...

What the Spanish Government and investigators do not seem to appreciate with us foreigner investigators, is that we are not stealing their work; instead we are helping to clean up Spain of all the foreign bad guys and work that they could not do because of the language barriers, customs and traditions.

As I only deal with the foreigners, in my case the English and German are the bad guys not the Spanish, and believe me there are enough bad guys for everyone. The Spanish are nearly as lazy as the English when it comes to learning another language, and they certainly could not deal with the foreign bad guys. So the Spanish government should really explain this to the investigators and make special allowances for the foreign investigators to be able to work in Spain; and be happy that we are helping keep some of the bad guys out of Spain and sending them back to where they came from.

In the UK, private investigators have in the past never needed a license, as is the case in many other European countries. The British Home Office is the department that is responsible for these matters for the United Kingdom. Unfortunately this governmental department has been dragging its heels for the past few years — fifty years would be more the truth. Talking and talking about it, but doing nothing.

The British Home Office have shown in the past few years that they could not organise an egg-and-spoon-race with all their pomp and wisdom. I am sure licensing will come eventually; talk is now that in the year 2010 you will need a license as the security industry has become so enormous since the terrorists started their evil work. But what do you do about a PI that has worked for years and years, with only a couple of years to go before his pension, who then needs to start getting university degrees to get a license? Of course I am talking about me.

I know, I have a cheek to even talk about this subject as I still do not have my Spanish license though I am in the process of getting it; but there you go. The situation is now that I have been officially informed that I am working illegally in Spain, although I am a European Citizen with all the rights of the European Union. I could be charged at any time and when, and not if I am found guilty, would be heavily fined €3,000. If caught a second time working without a license, I could face imprisonment.

So it makes my work even more interesting. I am a bit too old to go back to school again but we shall see. So I will end the licensing issue here for now; but I will give you an update some time — if I have not been arrested by then and locked up that is.

25

Infidelity

This has to be one of the main things that spring to mind when you think of the words private investigator — infidelity —which is just the same old game as it ever was, but today modern cameras and GPS connections have lessened the chances of getting away with it.

Infidelity in Marbella

One of my first infidelity cases came to me through a private investigator from the south of England, requesting assistance in the form of surveillance of a 44-year-old Italian gentleman that was engaged to be married to a rather wealthy, or should I say *very* wealthy, English lady. The old problem of trust was of course the issue. You see this very good looking Italian gentleman had made several trips to Marbella in the south of Spain, alone without his fiancé, telling her that he was visiting his father, (who owned an Italian restaurant in the old town of Marbella,) and for some reason he always came home broke.

My partner for this trip was Rodolfo, a 60-year-old Italian national and retired colleague who was also a neighbour of mine in Cartagena. Rodolfo would often ride shot gun with me — when his wife allowed him to. Rodolfo had a good sense of humour and always laughed at my jokes, though I think it was more because of his lack or restricted knowledge of the English language that he always laughed; but he was good company.

As already mentioned every time the target, or "subject" as he is now known to us, travelled to Spain, he would after a few days telephone his fiancé with shocking news; telling her stories of how he had been mugged or that he had been pick-pocketed or robbed and either way he had no money and needed her help to financially fund his return trip to the UK from Spain. We shall call our subject Mr. X, for the sake of the story.

Mr. X's fiancée of course thought that he must be riding another woman on the side and wanted to know before marrying him if he was gentleman or a cheating cad.

Mr. X had worked as the chauffeur for his wealthy fiancée but because he complained of back problems he had not worked for her or any one else for the past three years; instead he conveniently enough lived off of his fiancée's wealth. I suppose you could call it early retirement.

Mr. X was to arrive on the Friday evening at Malaga International Airport and needed to be followed to see where he would be shacking up and more importantly, whom he was shacking up with.

I agreed a retainer with the agents and was sent all the necessary photos and paper work so that I would be able to travel down to Marbella the next morning, which would give me plenty of time to get to Malaga Airport and be in the arrivals hall to see the passengers arriving on Monarch Airways; Mr. X was to be one of them.

On Arriving at Malaga International Airport there was the same old traffic jams and chaos on the roads because of the construction of the new air terminal that was ongoing and supposed to have been finished being built a long time ago. It seemed that this terminal was being built for ever; I wondered if aeroplanes would still be in use when the airport would be finally finished or would they just beam people around; the new air-travel.

I did not have to wait very long before our man Mr. X came out with the other new arrivals, wearing very loud three quarter length Bahama shorts and a very colorful T-shirt, pulling a small travelling bag on wheels behind him. Mr. X, luckily for us, was 6' 6" tall, so he was easy enough to recognise amongst all the other colorful characters that were coming out of the arrival gate looking for the Spanish sunshine.

Mr. X had nobody to meet him at the airport and walked straight over to the taxi stand and jumped into a waiting taxi and off they went with me on a motorcycle in hot pursuit behind them.

I had been given the name of the hotel where Mr. X would be staying by the instructing agents, a 3-star hotel that really deserved no stars at all but it was a damn site better than having to sleep in the car again. Rodolfo had managed to get me us a room on the same floor as Mr. X, in the next room.

Thankfully it was late when Mr. X checked in at the hotel and he did not go out that night, so we could get some sleep.

The next morning Mr. X was up bright and early and said, "good morning," to me as he passed me on my observation point in the reception area of the hotel on his way to the beach. The beach was only five minutes walk from the hotel. Once on the beach, Mr. X started his morning exercises — making all kinds of poses and noises on the beach all by himself. There were only a few people on the beach at this early hour of the morning, 10:00 a.m.

It was important for me to fit into the back ground with my cameras at the ready, just waiting for the action. Plus there were some really pretty young ladies on the beach — all waiting to be discovered. And here I am, taking pictures of a 6' 6" Itai (Italian) man to make sure he was being a good boy. Now normally if he was screwing around he would have met his counterpart by now but nothing had happened; he had not even visited his father's restaurant. So what was going to be his next move? Maybe he was gay and waiting for his boyfriend?

I wasted my whole day watching this guy on the beach doing nothing except sun bathing. I was getting strange looks from some of the onlookers and waiters serving the sun bathers on the beach, as normally men would be looking at all the scantily clad female beauties exhibiting all they had to offer on the beach. There was me only interested in one ugly male, my 'target'.

4:00 p.m. — Mr. X takes a stroll back to the hotel and had not spoken to any body at all, all day. Rodolfo had checked out the father of Mr. X and he did indeed have an Italian restaurant, very small but in the very upmarket part of the old town in Marbella.

Rodolfo and I met up back at the hotel and took turns in observing our target's room to see if he would come out or if someone else would go in, but there was no movement to be seen.

At 1:00 a.m. we closed down our surveillance point for the night.

At around 3:00 a.m. we were awakened by a lot of noise coming from downstairs in the hotel reception area. Rodolfo and I got up to see what was going on and we were very surprised to see that our target was the centre of attraction, in a verbal argument with the night watchman. Things were getting ugly and the night watchman was an old man in his 70's so we went to his aid. When I asked what the hell was going on our target immediately backed off and went back to his room.

I asked the night watchman what the problem was and he was very busily thanking us for intervening as he was clearly shaking with fear. Again I asked what was going on here. It did not take too long before our curiosity was appeased.

The night watchman was only to happy to tell us how the man (our target) had stayed in the hotel before and that he would lose all his money gambling in the casino; then he would sneak out of the hotel without paying, leaving his father to pick up the tab. Now he was just about to do the same thing again.

Our target had a 'compulsory gambling disorder'. He constantly lost everything he had in the casino and would then invent a sad story for his future wife to come to the rescue.

It was now 4:15 a.m. and we went back to our room telling the night-watchman that if he had any more trouble to call us and we would come down and sort it out.

It was too early to contact our client and I fell asleep in minutes.

9:30 a.m. — I received a telephone call from our agent in the UK.

"Have you monitored all the action?!" he yelled through the telephone.

"Oh yes we have," I said proudly.

"And are the police there, or is the target in hospital?" he asked.

"Well no. The target is in his room and there have been no visits from the police or anyone else," I replied.

The agent in London was getting angry now.

"Did you see who mugged him? Did you see the traffic accident?"

"Not at all. What are you talking about" I asked.

The agent then went on to explain that the target had called his wife-to-be and said that a car rammed his hired car and then three men attacked him and robbed him of all his money, watch and passport taken from him.

I assured the London agent that the target was still in his room, that he did not have a hired car and certainly had not been involved in a car accident or mugging. There was a short silence.

"What the hell is going on?" the agent said, probably wondering if we were in the *right* hotel, following the *right* target.

At that moment I could hear the target talking very loudly on the telephone.

"Listen darling I need some money to get home and pay the hotel. Call me back in five minutes I must have a poo first (go to toilet in baby language) and then you can tell me what you have arranged," and with that he ended the telephone call.

We were rolling over with laughter in the next room thinking of him going for his poo.

I also found out that the casino heavies were out looking for Mr. X.

I explained to the agents in London that the target had a history here in Marbella and that he had a compulsory gambling disorder. Our report and photos would be sent to London within ten minutes, from my laptop.

Infidelity on Tenerife

A friend of mine in Tenerife was given the instruction to video a lady's husband for a full day on a Sunday that she visited her mother, expecting her husband to be screwing around with every woman in town. On the Sunday in question the husband came outside his house in overalls paint and paint brush in his hands and painted the window frames of the house all day long.

Now that is what the mistrusting wife got to see on her video report. Her husband painting window frames from early morning till nightfall. And for that she was billed and had to pay £650.

She was not happy with the result but it was a result; not the one she wanted, but a result just the same.

26

The Crying Policeman

I have heard of the "laughing policeman" but I was very surprised to meet a "crying policeman".

I had to process serve an ex-police officer who had locked himself in his house and refused to come out. When I arrived at the man's property, the neighbours were all gathering in front of the house in little groups and. As I walked towards the front gate of the house, I was immediately challenged by a rather old and obese lady. "Who are you and what do you want?" I was asked in not-so-friendly tone of voice.

I looked at around and counted nine people standing around.

"Excuse me but what is going on here?" I said.

The obese lady looked at me again.

"It's that poor man again; he has locked himself in his house and has threatened to commit suicide."

"Oh well," I said, "then maybe I am just in time."

"In time for what?" said the obese lady.

"Excuse me; is there anyone here that is a close friend of the gentleman that I can speak to?"

A lady and man came forward and said, "We are close friends of the ex-policeman. Who are you?"

I showed my badge and ID card and asked them to come away from the crowd and speak with me.

The obese lady was a bit upset to be left out as she wanted to be in on everything, but it was none of her business anyway.

"I am here to personally hand some documents to the gentleman in the house. Please can you explain the situation to me; what is going on here?"

The man spoke first. "I had to break into the house this morning and try and talk sense to the man; but he will not listen. His wife left him three years ago and he cannot get over it. Ever since that time he has been threatening to kill himself. We have called the police and the ambulance several times and they came but nothing has been done.

"So this man has been holding the whole street to ransom by threatening to kill himself," I said.

"Yes that's about the size of it. He is an ex-policeman and he gets very rude, and when I spoke to him this morning he told me to piss off," the man said.

The lady interrupted. "Please, if you have any papers for him, can you not give them to us, and we can give them to him another day?"

"No, I am sorry but I am not allowed to do that. But you can please tell him that I was there and that I will be back to visit him tomorrow," I said then took my leave of the neighbours and drove back to my office.

I contacted my instructing solicitor, explained the situation and requested a substituted service. (This is when we know that the person is there but for some reason will not accept the papers personally and we have to entrust the papers to a third party, or leave the documents in the letter box.) My instructing client spoke with the judge in the case and managed to change the order to a substituted service.

The next day I returned but this time there were no neighbours waiting outside the house and to my amazement the ex-policeman was sitting in his front garden enjoying a drink! The front gate was open and I asked if I might enter the garden. The ex-policeman beckoned me to come in. I could not believe the size of the man; he was fatter and rounder than he was tall.

"Hi my name is Rick" I offered him my hand and he shook it. "And what can I do for you young man?" he said in a pleasant manner. I said that I was a process server and that I had some court documents for him and at the same handed him the sealed envelope with the documents. He opened the envelope and took one look at the papers, and that set him off.

"I am an ex-police officer and I am telling you to go to hell and that I do not accept these papers; so fuck off!" he shouted at me, while throwing the papers into the street from his sitting position. I politely said, "I am also an ex-police officer and the documents have been served correctly on you."

I then picked the papers up from the street and put them on his pathway. I really did not expect this outburst of abuse from the man but I was even more surprised when I looked back at the man and he was crying like a little baby. We had everything documented on camera. Inga had been busy taking the pictures of the action from inside the back of my car.

I felt sorry for the poor fellow, but he had created his own situation. I telephoned the neighbours the next day to see if there had been anymore threats of suicide or if he had even chopped himself. The good neighbours said that everything had quietened down since my visit and that the man was now being reasonable. Whatever I had said to him "did some good" as he was now on talking terms with everybody and out walking his dogs!

Apparently he had not taken his dogs for a walk in three years!
Poor doggies!

27

A Dangerous, Nasty, Big Man

I received instructions to serve a high court restraining order on a rather unsavoury person in a town only 40 miles away from where I lived, with a penal notice (the penal notice means that the person served can be arrested and go to prison if he does not abide by the court order).

In my instructions I was informed that past process servers had physical problems with this man and he would avoid being served. If the subject was not at his home address then he could be found in the local bars in the area, as he also had a drinking problem.

At midday I drove to the address that was supplied to me as being where the man lived, but there was nobody at home. I saw that there were several pairs of shoes on the doorstep to the house so somebody must be home. But there was not a sign of the subject or anybody else around that I could ask where the man might be. After ten minutes I walked around to some of the English named bars, where the subject would most likely be. The first two bars were closed but the third was open and so I went inside and ordered a cup of tea.

"Do you know Chris James?" I asked the barman,
"Everybody knows him," the barman said.
"Where do you think I could find him now?"
"Oh he will be in his bed sleeping it off more than likely. He

was here until three this morning and he had a skinful."

"Thanks very much," I said drank my tea and left walking off in the direction of my car.

After half an hour I went back to the house of Mr. James to see if he was now at home or maybe just getting up. There had been no re-arrangement of the shoes on the door step so I decided to take a photo of the house and then go back to my office. Just as I had my camera positioned to take a photo I felt a shadow come over me from behind. I turned around to see this huge man, tattooed from head to foot. He could have been the understudy for Mr. Universe, wearing just a pair of boxer shorts.

"Hey, what the fuck are you doing?" he yelled at me in an unmistakable East London accent!

"Hello, are you Mr. James?!

"Yes. What's that to you and why are taking fucking photo of my 'ouse?"

"My name is Rick and I am a process server from the English court and I have some documents for you sir."

"Who you looking for? James, never heard of 'im. Now give me that fucking camera."

I said that it was not a problem if he was not Mr. James and I would just take the papers back with me, but as for my camera, no way was I going to give it to him!

I walked away towards my car, wishing I had someone covering me with a shot gun, or at least to photograph me just as I was about to be beaten to death by this huge, tattooed, nasty man.

As I climbed into my car I felt a sense of security around me. Mr. James started shouting abuse at me from across the road where he was standing and then he shouted,

"Let me ave a look at them papers."

I drove over to where Mr. James was standing and as I slowed down he made a lunge at me through my open car window. I was holding some of the papers in my left hand. He snatched them and started to hit me in the face with them at the same time! In a reflex-like movement I threw all the other papers out of my car window into the street and put my foot down on the gas pedal.

I stopped after about ten yards and looked at the man picking his scattered papers up from the ground.

With a loud clear voice I said, "Mr. James you have been served," and then I left like a bat out of hell.

28

The Story of One-Eyed John

I met Big Jon in a café in Alicante after he had telephoned me about some domestic problems that he was having with his younger wife, 30 years his junior.

John had been married seven years with a pretty young lady half his age. John from southern England was 6' 6" tall, a gentle giant and well built for a man in his 60's.

(This was another domestic case where the younger wife had found a younger man and it was all really down to vulnerability and availability.)

When I met John he refused to speak in front of Inga so she had to leave the café and wait in the car; she was not happy about it at all. Then I noticed that there was something not quite right with John's left eye lid; every few seconds it looked as if he was winking at me. I tried to concentrate on John's story but it was difficult as I could not stop looking at his winking eye. From that day on we called our client 'one eyed John'.

I had a long consultation with John and noted down his instructions. He paid me a decent retainer and I thought this would be a one or two-day job. But whenever I think it's going to be an easy job it will be a hard job; think it will be quick it will take a long time, so I really never know the story until it unveils.

Over the seven years of marriage John had had problems with his wife before and they had split up a couple of times, but in the end he forgave her and they re-united. There are of course always two sides to a story and I was getting paid just to hear one side.

Three months later and we were still on the same job; not for the whole three months but a day here and a week-end there. We had gathered all the evidence and video footage required and met with Big Jon to finish up.

John was so upset when he saw the evidence and although he called his wife every evil name under the sun he still loved the woman.

I felt sorry for Big Jon and so I invited him to come with me to Marbella for a change of scenery. I had a process service to carry out and I thought John would be good company for me for the long drive down to Marbella and back.

One Big Mistake

Take my advice; if you have a long journey ahead of you and you want to help someone, never invite a manic depressive love-sick person along for the ride. I had to learn this the hard way.

During this journey, I heard his life story several times and how many times his wife had been untrue to him and if I stopped the car to get fuel, Jon would say, "I was here with my wife some time ago." When I stopped for a coffee, he said, "I was here with my wife..." This went on, all the bloody way to Marbella!

When we reached Marbella I said, "Jon let's go into the old town of Marbella it's really nice, and Puerto Banus, the famous marina with its luxury sailing yachts and multi-millionaire motor cruisers and the jet set."

Jon said, "That's where we had our honeymoon." There was no way I could get Jon to talk about anything other than his wife so I gave up and just nodded in agreement for the return trip.

The trip took three days and when I delivered Jon back to where he had left his car in Alicante, he thanked me and said it did him good to get away from his problems for a couple of days. I could not figure out how he had managed it, as it had been an ongoing trip down memory lane from start to the end of the trip. I was happy to get away from him and go back home.

Two days later Big Jon called me in a very happy mood, the woman he would have loved to have put through a mincemeat machine wanted to come back to him.

"Oh that's great, Jon," I said. But there was little problem; his wife was to break off the affair she had been in for the past three months. Big Jon's wife was scared that her lover would make trouble. He wanted me to go and wait in a hotel bar with three heavies, in case the lover became nasty and aggressive. If her (now) ex-lover did get out of order we were to protect his wife.

"OK, Jon, when and where?" I said.

"To morrow midday at a well known hotel in Alicante," he said.

I gave him a price of €450 and Jon reluctantly agreed. He thought it was to be a freebie; but I explained I had to pay the other three men's costs and travel expenses.

"OK, OK but if the perpetrator gets nasty, just pin him to the ground, and kick him once in his privates from me. I will be waiting outside the hotel and she will get into my car once she has told him that it is all over and that she is returning to her husband. She will then come out of the hotel and we will then drive off. I don't want him trying to stop her or running after her."

"OK Jon. All understood."

The next day I was in the hotel bar with three of my men as arranged drinking coffee; we waited for over an hour and then Big Jon's wife arrived with her ex-lover-to-be. We sat one table away from them just waiting for the trouble to start. I saw Big Jon's car outside.

Big Jon's wife stood up and with out saying goodbye, walked off to the entrance of the hotel and did not look back. We stood up and made our way to the entrance of the hotel expecting any minute for something to happen — but it didn't. Big Jon's wife got into Jon's car and they drove off. We all looked at each other, when just then the ditched lover boy came out of the hotel and sat on the steps of the hotel entrance with his hands buried deep into his face and burst out crying.

And that was it — "case closed".

One eyed Jon called me six months later to tell me that he had now divorced his wife and that they had an amicable financial settlement. Jon asked if I would be going down to Malaga again soon and I said no, unfortunately I do not do that run anymore...

Best of luck, Jon.

29

Traces with Happy faces

As you can imagine a lot of a private investigator's work is to find missing people for many reasons, and more bad reasons than good. The majority of trace work is to locate people who have run away from their problems or debts and are of the opinion that if they start a new life in Spain that no one will ever find them again; how wrong they are.

I have a 96% hit rate on finding missing persons.

We have to be very careful when a client asks us to carry out a trace, to both protect the target that needs to be traced and ourselves, from assisting a potential bad guy who may have very bad intentions in store for the target being traced. We also have to be absolutely sure who the client is, and for what reason the person is to be traced.

In some cases the person being traced has the right to know that they are being traced and can decide themselves if they want to let the person tracing them know where they are or not. But it's not a good idea if the subject has run off owing a fortune to somebody to let them have that decision.

New York, New York

Recently I received an enquiry to trace someone for a well known group of London solicitors; to locate a gentleman who had just inherited a fortune. I found the man in question in Malaga and he was of course very happy about being found and more so because he was now a richer man than he was before I knocked on his door.

One night I received a telephone call from New York at about 2:00 a.m. in the morning; and I am not the friendliest person at that hour. A lady called me and judging by her voice a rather senior lady, requesting a trace to be carried out on another lady that she knew 44 years ago. I wondered what the connection could be as the lady kept telling me that it was her "chica," meaning her girl.

The potential client's name was Mrs. Stone from Manhattan and she was not related to her Chica, who she wanted me to find. Mrs. Stone told me that four private investigators had worked on the trace previously in the past with no success and she then went on to say that she was herself 85 years old and she prayed that she would see her Chica before she died.

Mrs. Stone went on to say how Chica was her best friend and how she had worked for her when Mrs. Stone lived in Madrid over 40 years ago; but when she returned to Manhattan she lost all contact with Chica.

I told Mrs. Stone that I would do my best but she should not hold her breath. To cut a long story short the only thing I had to go on was a condolence card with 15 names signed on it. Mrs. Stone found the Spanish condolence card amongst some old papers that she had in a much travelled suit case, I asked Mrs. Stone to send it over to me with my retainer. I received the card and retainer a week later. Looking at the condolence card I found Chica's name signed on it but no surname. So this was my clue; a condolence card that was at least 40 years old and a Spanish Christian name.

I looked at each name on the card and then I systematically searched for every name that had signed with a surname. I traced a relative of Chica's from the card and I hit lucky and established Chica's now married name. She married a Frenchman, immigrated and lived in France for ten years; and then with her husband and children she returned to Madrid.

I telephoned Chica to ask her if she knew Mrs. Stone and if she would like to meet her. At first Chica was reluctant as she did not know me so I arranged a meeting with her.

Inga and I travelled to Madrid to meet Chica, now a 79-year-old Spanish senior citizen. Chica was very suspicious of me at first and didn't want to believe what I said about Mrs. Stone. But after I had told her the story and Mrs. Stone' dying request she smiled and allowed me to photograph her for Mrs. Stone; and she readily agreed to contact Mrs. Stone so that the two old friends could meet up again after so many years.

I telephoned Mrs. Stone in New York and informed her of our good luck and Mrs. Stone was just overwhelmed with happiness and excitement and she telephoned her Chica the same day.

Two weeks after my meeting with Chica in Madrid, Mrs. Stone invited Inga and I to meet her and Chica during the holiday in Madrid. She also said because I had succeeded in making an old lady so happy by tracing and finding her Chica, she had a special surprise for me, 'all the way from New York'.

I must say that I was excited to meet these happy people, and also to find out what my surprise was that was coming 'all the way from New York'. I drove six hours to get to the Holiday Inn Hotel in Madrid. After Inga and I had checked in to the hotel, we went to reception to meet Mrs. Stone and Chica.

I found Mrs. Stone in the middle of a group of rather senior citizens, all ladies busily chatting away. I approached the group and saw Chica but before I had a chance to introduce myself a huge, and I mean huge, 85-year-old lady yelled,

"You must be Rick!"

I humbly replied, "Yes that's me."

"Come here my boy," Mrs. Stone said. I put my outstretched hand to greet Mrs. Stone but my hand was pushed to one side as Mrs. Stone said, "This is what I have for you, all the way from New York, my boy" and she bear hugged me so hard that I could hardly breathe.

So that was the surprise from New York; a bear hug from an 85-year-old great grandmother! After the three-minute bear hug, we all went for coffee and drinks together.

I was even more surprised that when I checked out of the hotel; €93 Euros had been added to my bill, being all the drinks that Mrs. Stone, Chica and friends had enjoyed at my expense.

Mrs. Stone had paid well so I could not complain and the success and achievement of the job gave me such satisfaction. I was happy and I learnt another valuable lesson:

Be wary of New Yorkers!

30

USA Rape Trial

A man was in jail in California and had been charged with the rape of a 30-year-old Scottish lady called Susan. The case was now at trial and the man had been in custody for already six months, with bail refused by the courts. The case was coming to an end, when Susan, the Scottish lady, was giving her testimony in the witness box to the court.

Susan started crying and shocked the court when she said, "This is not the first time that I have been had the misfortune of being raped and I will never trust a man again." Immediately the defense lawyers picked up on what she had told the court and asked her where she had been raped before and by whom.

Susan now very upset, told the defense lawyer that she had lived in Barcelona for a short time and that an Indian man had raped her after she accepted an invitation to go to his apartment one evening. Susan was not alone that night; she was with a friend who was also the girlfriend of the Indian man's brother, so she thought it would be OK.

After they arrived at the apartment, Susan's girlfriend went to the bedroom with her boyfriend and they were busy having sex. Then the older brother came on to Susan and raped her in the front room of the apartment. Susan went on to tell the court that after she had been raped she managed to get away from the man and out of the apartment and alarm the police. Susan was then taken to a hospital in Barcelona and the Indian man was arrested and charged with raping her. He was tried by the Barcelona criminal courts and found guilty of raping Susan. The man received ten years in prison after admitting to raping Susan.

The defense lawyers requested a recess adjournment of three days, which the judge granted. I was telephoned by the defense lawyers and they said that I had been recommended by a law firm in New York. I was impressed. Was *that* the old lady's surprise?

I was required at once to go to Barcelona and to confirm the story that Susan had told the court. After receiving my instructions by email and my retainer via Western Union, I travelled by train to Barcelona. I had now spoken with the defense lawyers in the USA several times a day, and the defense lawyer said that he could not believe that this Scottish lady would be so unlucky as to get raped in every country that she went to.

I met a Spanish colleague of mine, David San Martin, when I arrived in Barcelona and together we looked into the mystery rape of Susan. I say 'mystery rape' because that's exactly what it was. There was no report in any newspapers, TV, radio, police or hospital and no records whatsoever of an Indian man raping a poor, harmless, 22-year-old Scottish lady called Susan. Also, Susan could not provide the court with any names or addresses of where her sex attack took place.

After two days I called the defense lawyers in California with the negative results of our investigation in Barcelona. Next I needed to write my report and swear an affidavit, and send it DHL to California as quick as possible.

The defense lawyers put me on standby to fly out to California, to give evidence in court. I had seen in the movies how the lawyers tear private investigators apart in court, so I was not looking forward to the prospect of having to go and testify.

Ten days later I was more than relieved to receive a call from the defense lawyers telling me that the judge had accepted my evidence in court and that I would not be required to attend.

In the witness box Susan was cross-examined using the evidence that I had sent. She told the court that the Indian man paid a financial settlement and that she withdrew the charges and that the man was deported to India.

With this latest bullshit story Susan had once again shot herself in the foot. When criminal charges have been brought against somebody, only the state department of public prosecution, represented by the general attorney's office, can decide to withdraw the case or not.

The case was thrown out of court in California and the man released from jail. Susan was charged and deported back to the United Kingdom for making false allegations and wasting police time.

31

Process Serving at a Travellers' Site

Another interesting process service.

I had received a statuary demand to deliver personally to a man who "lived in the tranquil olive groves somewhere in Malaga". I had traced the man some months earlier and now the papers had arrived for personal service. The town I had to visit was called 'Monte Frio' or Cold Mountain.

Inga and I drove down to Cold Mountain and to our disappointment we could not find the address where the target lived so I stopped a police car from the Guardia Civil and asked if they could help me find the address. I showed my detective badge and explained that I had court papers to deliver at the address. The police were very concerned and asked me to come into the police station with them that was just around the corner.

Inga and I went into the police station and were invited to look into the police computer and found our target's address. The police knew something that I didn't; and that this was a travellers' halting site.

The gypsies are well known wherever they go, and not for the best reasons.

The police insisted that they take us to the travellers' halting site in a police jeep and I happily accepted. After a 25-minute drive through the olive grove tracks, (no roads,) we arrived at the small encampment. I would never have found this place in a million years on my own.

When I got out of the police car and asked where a Mr. Simpson was, the people just looked at me with blank expressions on their faces. Small children running around totally naked and old women sitting on white plastic chairs had a look of vengeance against society written all over their faces

Then a voice shouted out, "I am Simpson. Who wants to know?"

And then I saw this very large and obese man come out of a caravan. Just to look at this man was scary, with his long hair, earrings in both ears and scruffy rough looks. He had a strange smile on his dirty face as he saw the two armed policeman standing either side of me. Meanwhile, Inga was busy taking photographs from the back seat of the police jeep for evidence of service.

I looked at the big man and said, "Hi Mr. Simpson. I am a process server and I have some papers for you sir from the English courts," as I put them in his hand and wished him good luck. I turned around and climbed back into the police jeep. I noticed how all the eyes watched every move we made as we slowly drove off down the track again and back to the village of Monte Frio.

I was so grateful to the local police; they were absolutely great, and this process service I am sure, would not have been peaceful or even possible with out their help.

I think that we were the sensation of the day in the village of Monte Frio, as not much really ever happens in the small villages. I invited the police for coffee and had a long talk about our work in Spain.

The photographs were first class and were presented in court as evidence another job well done.

32

The Lettuce Patch

Who would ever think that lettuce could be of mega importance, and worth millions of dollars?

I have been very lucky to be living in the part of Spain known as the "garden of Spain" where until a few years ago the town of Los Alcazares was surrounded by open fields with citrus fruit and all kinds of vegetables. Due to local housing construction boom a lot of the fields were changed into ugly looking building sites, and golf courses. The plantations are no longer open because of foreign migrants from Europe helping themselves to each and every thing they could carry as if they were starving. Today sadly all the fruit and vegetable plantations are closed off with high wire fences. No wonder the farmers were happy to sell out to the construction companies, with the unprecedented petty stealing that went on by the new wave of residents.

One day, a 52-year-old English farm manager who had lived in the area for the same number of years as myself, called me to come over to his farm, as he had a problem that needed to be investigated.

The farm was only 25 kilometres from my office so it only took me a few minutes to drive over and as I drove there I passed field after field of lettuces.

This was very big 250-acre agricultural farm that grew only lettuce and nothing else and as I drove nearer to the farm office to meet the farm manager it became quite clear how large the farm land really was.

Figure 3 *The lettuce patch*

The farm manager was waiting for me and on arrival he introduced himself as Ted. We talked about his problem: Ted had sold and transported lettuce, for one and half million Euros, to the United Kingdom; he delivered all the big supermarkets, which were long standing customers of his. So far so good, until a customer from Tesco's in England complained that she had found broken glass in the lettuce head that she had just bought from Tesco and of course demanded her money back. Tesco immediately checked all the freshly delivered lettuce that had arrived from Spain and discovered that there was more broken glass pushed deep into the heart of other lettuce heads.

This situation now turned really nasty and became a very dangerous, if a child or anyone had swallowed the glass or choked on it, it was just too terrible to even think about what could happen to them, apart from the farm going bankrupt as a result.

The farm manager went on to tell me that he had some 75 foreign workers, mostly from Morocco, and some of the men were "illegals," meaning that they had no work permits and were possible illegal immigrants as well.

Ted had problems some months back with four of the workers because they were late for work or did not turn up at all, and so he fired them. The farm manager explained that he had to run a tight ship otherwise the workers would do what ever they wanted.

I asked him if he had reported the matter to the Spanish police and he said that he had and that they showed no interest at all. I did not really believe that Ted had reported the matter to the police, because of all the illegal manpower that he employed.

I visited the beautiful green and red lettuce fields on the 250-acre farm with Ted the farm manager. I cut several lettuce heads and put them in a plastic bag to look at them more closely. In three of the lettuce heads I found broken brown beer bottle glass that had been deliberately pushed into the heart of the lettuce — this was obviously with malicious intent.

Ted told me that he had lost his whole year's harvest and that none of his customers were interested in buying from him until he could prove that his products were no longer contaminated. Ted had also been informed that several other corporate customers had also complained of glass in the lettuce heads that they had received from him.

Ted did not know which way to turn with his problem; was it the disgruntled foreign workers, or could it be the competition that was doing this?

My problem was how to control 250 acres of farm land and lay a trap to catch the perpetrators? I had to go back to my office and somehow calculate a quotation for Ted, without shocking him too much.

One thing was already clear in my mind and that was that I would need more man power so I called around to my contacts and within a couple of hours I had six men ready to act if required.

There were two plans of action; one was to interview the foreign workers and to scare the shit out of them individually, saying that an informant had come forward and that we knew the persons involved, and hope that someone would panic. The other way was the hard way and that meant running patrols day and night 24/7 until we caught the perpetrators red handed, and that was going to be highly unlikely.

I quoted a ball park figure to Ted, (with no guarantee of success,) of what it would cost him for five to six days work with seven agents. Ted very reluctantly agreed and I promised to start first thing in the morning.

Back in my office I telephoned Daniel to organise the manpower and said that two of the agents should be able to speak Arabic, and two others should be wearing grey suits, collar and tie and also to come in two identical BMWs.

8:00 am the next morning, Daniel was at my office to meet me and to discuss the plan of action. The object was to interview each and every farm worker and to try and get the perpetrators denounced. We were not impersonating the police, but it had to look like we were some kind of government officials to get the results we wanted.

Ted had informed his workers that they were to be interviewed before they went to work in the fields again. The tension was really high and even more so when we arrived. I had blue flashing lights that we put on the roof of the BMW cars, so that our entrance really attracted attention.

Once on the farm I commandeered the farm manager's office to conduct the interviews with the workers. I had one of the translators with me and the two grey suited agents and Daniel took the other two agents to photograph the farm land. I had a small plastic bag with broken brown glass in it along with some papers spread neatly across the table.

We told each worker that he had nothing to worry about if he told the truth, but if he was found to be telling lies he would be deported. And to know anything and not reveal it to us was a criminal offence, which would make him as guilty as the person who did it.

The questions were:
1. How long have you worked on this farm?
2. How long have you been in Spain?
3. Do you like living in Spain?
4. Do you like the farm manager?
5. Would you like to stay and work on the farm?
6. How long have you been illegally in Spain?
7. Have you ever seen the broken glass like in this plastic bag before?
8. We have found finger prints on the glass do you have any objection if we take your finger prints?
9. Do you know who put the broken glass in the lettuce heads?
10. Do you know this terrible damage to the lettuce heads could well kill someone maybe an innocent child, and then the charge would be murder?

Then we said to each man:

"We have another room where you can speak to one of the investigators in Arabic if there is anything you would like to tell us. We already have certain information but we are giving you the chance to come clean; if you cooperate with our investigation you will not be deported."

The interviewing was very slow and the men were very tight lipped and the faces were expressionless.

We had now interviewed 12 men and it was already 6:00 p.m. so I suggested that we close and start again the next day. In the meantime I organised a car to patrol the fields for the first night.

So far all our efforts were for nothing but we would have to wait and see as in the meantime the men would have plenty of time to talk to each other.

Ted had received more calls, this time from Morrison's, another customer, complaining about glass in the lettuce that they had received and it was all to be destroyed.

Day 2

We started the interviews at 8:00 a.m. and after interviewing another five suspects we stopped for a break. One of the reasons that the questioning was taking so long was that none of the worker spoke Spanish, only Arabic.

The word was out that everybody was now a suspect, and you could cut the tension with a knife.

The field patrols had nothing new to report except that glass had been found now in every one of the fields. There were no car tracks or even bicycle tracks to be found by the fields, so our man or men must be on foot.

Whoever was doing the damage knew very well what they were doing, almost professional, I would say.

The days interviewing came and went with again no results — except that five men did not turn up for work.

Day 3

I asked Ted if he had the addresses of the five men that never turned up for work the day before and Ted pointed to an old shack at the end of one of the lettuce fields. All the foreign workers lived in five shacks; they were not with their families, just here for the harvest season and then most of them returned to North Africa.

I asked Daniel to take over the interviewing a I wanted to go with the field patrol to look at the shacks, to see if I could find the five men that had not turned up for questioning.

I was amazed to see how simple the workers lived in this very primitive housing. Open fires to cook on and no electricity. All the shacks had two wells, for water and their toilets. Then there was a spade lying dormant against the wall of the shack.

The first three shacks were empty of people but in the fourth I found two of the male workers, in bed enjoying each other. When they saw me they jumped up like rabbits.

"Why did you not come to work yesterday?" I said.

"No speak Engleeesh," was the reply.

I called in Mohammed who was waiting in the car. He looked very shocked as he saw the two men.

"What is the problem Mohammed?"

"If the other workers find out that these men are homosexual they will certainly kill them," Mohammed said.

"Oh well, only we know that at the moment, do we not? Please tell the two men that I need an answer right now, otherwise I will have no other option than to inform their workmates of the situation of them being lovers."

After this was communicated to the two men, I listened to some whining for about five minutes.

"Well that's it, we must be off. Have a nice day," I had interpreted for the two men. Now one of them was begging, on his knees to me, tugging at my shirt.

"Answers; that's all I want, answers," I said as I looked down at the two poor souls.

Mohamed looked at me with pity and said, "You know you are passing down the death sentence on them if you inform their work mates." I looked at the men again, and then looking at Mohamed said, "I want answers; nothing more and nothing less."

The two men started speaking at the same time to Mohamed and I waited for Mohamed's interpretation.

Mohamed said that all the men knew about what was going on in the plantation but they wanted nothing to do with it. The planting of the broken glass was in retaliation for Moslem workers being publicly humiliated in front of all the other workers.

"I want names of the men who planted the glass and evidence," I said to Mohamed.

"The perpetrators are from another farm and are no longer in Spain," the sorry men said.

"Sorry, not good enough. I need names," I said. "But I will give twenty-four hours to find out the names. Otherwise you leave me no other option. If you do not give me the names by this time tomorrow, then you know what I will have to do."

The evidence was very quickly found at the back of the last shack: a mountain of broken beer bottles. "But the Moslems do not drink," I said "Oh but some do," Mohamed said.

The broken glass that I found at the back of shack 5 was identical to the glass found in the lettuce heads.

In the last shack I found three more workers but they were not sleeping or messing with each other. They said that they had cleaning and cooking duties for the other men that were working. Mohamed confirmed that was the norm. I took some photographs of the mountain of broken glass and the shacks before leaving to return to the farm.

It was a good day's work. I had established the motive and found the evidence but I still did not have the names.

6:00 p.m. — Back in the farm office Daniel had interviewed another six suspects, but they were just as tight lipped as the others before them.

I asked Daniel to come with me and the farm manager for a case meeting and. I informed them of what I had found out and we discussed and planned our way forward for the next day. The workers were aware that the questioning would continue and I think that they were very scared, but not scared enough to come out and tell us the truth.

The next morning we started by questioning the five suspects that had not turned up for work the day before, which included our two gay guys.

We questioned the men one at a time as soon, and as the interview was over I gave them a card with my telephone number saying that any information anonymously given would be discreetly dealt with.

The night patrols were really a waste of time so I instructed the two patrol agents to close down at midnight. So the workers did not know if the agents were there all night or not.

We are now into our fourth day and still more than 30 suspects to question, just waiting for a breakthrough. In the afternoon I called the two gay workers back into the office for questioning again. Daniel was to my right and Mohamed to my left.

I looked the two men straight in their faces.

"What names do you have for me and what proof," I asked in a sympathetic fashion. Shyly the older of the two men handed me a rather dirty crumpled passport photograph and said nothing.

I asked Mohamed to ask who this was in Arabic; the reply was: "the man who put the glass in the lettuce."

What's his name?" I asked. No reply so I asked again but Mohamed said, "They cannot say or do any more than give you the photograph."

"I understand; you can go back to work now and do not worry, no more will be said," I said to the two men, who then left the office.

I asked Daniel to continue with the interviews as I had to speak with Ted to see if he recognised the face on the photograph. The questioning had to continue so that no one would suspect another of talking with us.

Ted recognised the face on the photograph as one of the men he had fired some months ago and he still had the name on file but no address. I said to Ted, "It's now a matter for the Spanish police. We can give them the evidence that we have; but I cannot give the names of the workers that gave me the photograph, only a statement that is not signed."

I informed Ted that we must continue with the interviews until every worker had been questioned so that no suspicion would fall upon our two informants (only Mohamed, Daniel and myself knew about the two gays and that is how it would stay).

Saturday midday we were finished with all the interviews and we thanked all the workers for their great cooperation. The workers looked at each other rather puzzled and then the Spanish police arrived in two squad cars. The workers seemed relieved that we would soon be leaving, but when the police got out of the squad car and came over to me and shook my hand the relieved faces changed to panic stricken again.

I went into the farm manager's office with Ted, Daniel, Mohamed and the Spanish police and I informed the police of what we had established on the case and gave them the photograph.

The police recognised the man on the photograph as being arrested for snatching an old ladies handbag at Murcia Airport and he was still in custody, awaiting a deportation order.

The police asked Ted if he wanted to press charges against the man and I advised Ted not to as the suspect most certainly did not have any money to pay for all the damage he had caused and he was to be deported, so end of the problem. Ted agreed and the police were happy that they did not have to do any more work on such a beautiful sunny day.

I left with my men and the police followed us out of the farm yard; it did look very impressive. As far as I know Ted is back in business with no further problems on the plantation and I heard from Mohamed that the gays had split up and one has already returned to Morocco.

Oh yes, why the grey suits and identical BMWs?

For intimidation, of course.

Figure 4 The author with Daniel

33

Stone Crusher continued...
No Machine — No Case

I have often said before just when you think the job is done then you will most likely find out you were wrong. I thought that the stone crusher machine that we had located in the quarry in Durcal village, that had then been impounded by the Courts of Justice in Granada Spain and that were now under the responsibility of the Spanish police was dead and buried, but I was to be proved very wrong! Exactly one year ago to the day September 4th when I told you the story about the machine, I concluded that the stone crusher had now been impounded by the Guardia Civil and that the matter would have a happy end in the Spanish courts of justice!

I was wrong again... I received an email from Alejandro, the lawyer in Granada that was dealing with the case on behalf of my client in the USA, informing me that I should contact the client in the USA urgently, as there was a problem. I telephoned to ask him what the problem was all about, expecting to maybe have to appear in court to give evidence, but I was wrong again.

The lawyer was quickly on the telephone, "Rick there has been some confusion in the Courts in Granada." As he explained one of the judges was on vacation, and another judge had released the machine to Stefanie — "the bad guys" — as he had not seen the proof of ownership from our client that the machine belonged to him.

An application had been made to the court but the judge dealing with the case had not yet returned from his holidays and so as it stood, the machine could be collected by the bad guys and taken away. If there was no machine, there was no case, and they were totally legal to do so.

Hard to believe that this case had been in the Spanish courts for one year to decide the ownership of the machine and then a cock-up like this happens and nobody was in a hurry to correct this mistake!

I called my client in the USA .

"Hi Mark, this is Rick calling you from Spain — what do you need me to do here with this problem?" I asked. The reply came back, " Hell, the Court has screwed up" (or words to that effect!)

"I need you to go at once to stand guard on the machine again and if anyone moves it then follow it and do not let it out of your site "NO MACHINE — NO CASE".

I sent one of my men — Julio from Marbella — to drive over to where the stone crusher had been parked up for the past year, as he could be on site in Granada in one and half hours where as it would take me five hours to drive down to Granada from where I was based (in Cartagena).

The big yellow stone crusher was still parked up in the quarry where it had been impounded a year before; but now with no police guarding it, it could be collected and nothing could be done legally to prevent this.

Crime pays, doesn't it?

When I arrived in the village of Durcal I met Julio and we discussed how we would proceed if the bad guys showed up, then we took up surveillance positions so that we could clearly monitor the machine and if the machine received visitors.

It was a long and boring chilly Sunday night drinking cold coffee and looking at the stars.

But at 8 am the next morning things were already happening. I saw our old enemy Stefanie driving in an old blue Renault with a very large yellow low-loader lorry following her, driving up the mountain towards the quarry where the machine was.

I informed Alejandro, our Spanish lawyer, who instructed me to go to the police station in the village of Durcal and ask them to stop any-one from moving the machine from the quarry as the case of the machine was still pending a court decision.

The local police showed no concerns at all and said that they had to honour the courts decision that the bad guys had in their possession and to release the machine to them.

Our lawyers were hopeless and we were helpless — all we could do was to carry out our instructions and if the stone crusher was moved then we would have follow it where ever it may go, while our lawyers in the meantime try to get an injunction and court order to release the machine back to my client.

Julio and I waited all day for something to happen — we were now parked up just outside the quarry entrance. The local police arrived at the quarry and after twenty minutes or so left and returned to police HQ in the village; they visited the quarry owner just to make sure that we had behaved ourselves and not gone and snatched the stone crusher and run away with it.

8.15 pm — it was dark, cold and just about to rain when we heard the engines of the low-loader roaring and then we saw the huge truck driving down the mountain road-side with our precious stone crushing machine loaded up on the back, being followed by Stefanie and friends in her old blue Renault.

The low-loader turned left once it had left the mountain track in the direction of Granada and I slowly followed behind the low-loader with its yellow flashing warning lights spinning around letting everyone know the show had just began.

Julio was driving 5 miles behind me in another car (This is called leap frog tailing).

I was now driving immediately behind the low-loader with the yellow flashing lights shining straight into my face. Stefanie and a guy called Alejandro were driving in the Renault car behind me. I made it obvious that I was following the low-loader; the speed was 20 to 30 miles per hour. Then it started to rain. Did I say rain — no, it just bucketed down from the heavens, making driving conditions atrocious.

After an hour we were all on the main highway in the direction of Granada. I expected the low-loader to turn left in the direction of Malaga but I was wrong again! Instead of turning left to go to Malaga the low-loader turned right in the direction of Almeria being exactly the opposite of what I had anticipated.

The rain did not show any mercy on us and the only comforting thought I had, was knowing that the "bad guys" had the same shitty driving conditions as we did but they had the advantage of knowing where they were going and we didn't.

It was a long old drive and at 10.30 pm the low-loader pulled over to a highway truck stop hotel. We watched as the truck driver and the bad guys went into the restaurant and sat down to have their dinner. Julio had been keeping a low profile and had just joined me on the car park; he said that is usual in Spain to have dinner so late, they would be out in an hour or so. I was thinking this could be the same old trick the bad guys pulled off a year ago on a similar car park and while everybody was inside the restaurant eating, the stone crusher and the low-loader had disappeared from the car park. This was not going to happen again — not on my watch! After 3 hours I said "Julio they are having a very big dinner." They had finished their dinner in fact and taken a room in the hotel for the night.

9.30 am the next morning — the weather was still muggy and rainy and I had been up all night just waiting to see if the bad guys would try and pull a trick on me but they did not.

The truck driver came out followed by the bad guys and gave me a staring look and the driver started his truck and let the engines warm up for about 15 minutes before driving back onto the highway in the direction of Almeria.

The truck driver kept to all his legal stops for coffee breaks and was now driving in the direction of Cartagena. I remembered following the bad guys to a quarry the year before in Cartagena and it was only 20 miles from my home, so I was confident that would be where the stone crusher was to be taken to. I was so looking forward to going home for a good dinner and a shower but that was not to be.

We had now been driving some 350 miles at a snails pace of 25 miles an hour because the weather was so bad, the yellow flashing lights on the back of the low-loader were driving me nuts.

I informed our lawyer's in Granada of our progress and where we were and again they insisted that we call in the help of the police. I sent Julio on ahead to inform the highway patrol that we were following a stolen stone crusher and we needed assistance.

I felt good as I saw the two police men on their very impressive BMW motor cycles with blue flashing lights and sirens whaling away a bit like alligators going for the kill, the cops over-took the truck with the stone crusher and flag the driver down to follow them off the highway to a large car park and with and park up. With-in minutes there were three police cars, two police motor cycles, 9 policemen and one police woman on site looking at the papers from the Granada Courts that the bad guys had and discussing if they had discovered the crime of the century. After 25 minutes had passed and the crowds were gathering, to my complete surprise, the police gave permission for the low-loader to continue his journey and drive on!!! The police said there was nothing they could do as we did not have any court order to prove the contrary, and of course it made sense but it just did not make sense that the bad guys were getting away now — being assisted by the law.

Our lawyers had nothing prepared and we were now looking a bit stupid for asking police back up and stopping the low-loader. As the low-loader pulled off the car park I saw the smug grins on the faces of the bad guys who had certainly won this battle but not the war, or at least not yet.

Now for the short time we had stopped with the police the rain had stopped as well but now we were driving back on the highway and it was raining again. I was now only 65 miles from my office so I instructed Julio my fellow agent to follow the low-loader and I would drive to my office and hopefully pick up the Court order that our lawyers said they would email over to me. I got back to my office still thinking that the stone crusher would be taken to the Cartagena quarry and that I would be home for dinner and a bath.

Unfortunately there was no court order waiting for me on my computer when I arrived back at my office, only the court application that had not been processed by the court, so I grabbed it and called Julio on his cell car phone to find out their location Julio answered, "They are not going to Cartagena my friend! The truck has turned right onto another highway in the direction of Albacete and Madrid."

I was shocked to say the least — where the hell are they going to?

I ran to my car and with no time to lose drove off to try and find them again. I had a hard time to catch up but after an hour or so I saw the unmistakable yellow flashing warning lights of the low-loader and took my place behind the truck driving at a snails pace. The weather got from bad to worse. It was hard keeping awake but eventually I saw the road signs leading to Valencia, Tarragona and Barcelona. Oh no this just cannot be true, surely not Barcelona, that's a 1000 mile trip (one way).

The truck driver had to stop for a break at a truck stop café near to Valencia. Julio and I waited patiently outside the truck stop cafe prepared for any tricks that the bad guys may try to pull on us. We re-fuelled our cars and grabbed a sandwich and were ready to go again.

It did not take too long and we were back on the road in the direction of Barcelona. After another 6 hours of gruelling driving conditions the truck driver stopped for his well deserved coffee break. As the driver entered the truck stop café, I took advantage of this, taking some photographs of the stone crusher — that's when I noticed that some one at the same time was photographing me! The photographer was one of the bad guys and he looked at me and mumbled some thing in Catalan Spanish dialect that I didn't understand. Now Catalan is Spanish but a totally different Spanish language and I did not understand a word. I just smiled and said 'and bollocks to you, too'. He walked off back to the café, so I went into the café with Julio for a coffee. On entering the café I was approached by Stefanie. She asked me in very bad English what I had said to her companion out on the car park.

"Well", I said, "I asked him who he was."

"Well, he is Alejandro, the owner of the stone crusher," she proudly said. I recognised Stefanie's German accent and so I replied to her in German that we represented the true owner of the stone crusher.

Stefanie said that Mr. Alberto did not want any more trouble with this machine, he had really enough of one year of lawyer's fees and the stone crusher sitting idle not earning any money so she would like to propose a deal with my client in the USA to work together with them.

I looked into his beady little eyes. Alberto would be about 65 years old and by his own admission he suffered from a weak heart and sleeping sickness. I looked at his nicotine stained teeth — he possessed a shady look about him, like some one not to be trusted. He certainly looked a bit old and sick to be stealing stone crushing machines and selling them on again. But he certainly had no problem eating, as he was as round as he was tall.

I asked the bad guys where they were taking the stone crusher and Alejandro answered "to Tarragona." I said that I was not authorised to make any deals with them but I would certainly pass the message onto our lawyers and the real owner of the machine.

Stefanie was the 62 year old sister of Jochen, ring leader of the con organisation. Jochen had been caught and arrested in the USA and was in jail for a year waiting to be sentenced for grand fraud;

basically selling the same stone crushing machines again and again to as many people that he could con and this machine had been sold about three times already.

I was being nasty and I said to Stefanie, "did you know that your brother is in jail and that you will most likely follow him!"

She said at once, "I know nothing about the business that my brother did and I have nothing to do with any of it."

I looked at her and could see that she was scared shitless when I mentioned the word jail. Stefanie had blue eyes blond hair and a rather battered figure; obviously from many years of good eating. Originally from Austria, she had lived for about 20 years in Spain and spoke very good Spanish — but very bad English — she preferred her native tongue (German) so she was reasonable happy to speak with me. Alberto thought that I was an American and in some way related to my client the real owner of the machine my client Mark.

Time was getting on and as I saw the driver of the low-loader make his way to his low-loader we immediately all went to our respective cars to carry on the cat and mouse game.

We drove to Valencia and another 200 miles north to the outskirts of the city of Tarragona. The low-loader driver stopped at yet another truck stop café and went inside for his dinner. It was 10.30 pm. Stefanie and Alberto did not stop — they carried on to Barcelona. Julio parked up outside the truck stop café and then went inside while I waited out side the café.

The truck driver was neutral in all of the happenings that were going on and he told us that he would drive to the final destination in the morning about 50 miles north of Tarragona and then he would be finished once he had delivered the stone crusher to a yard on the industrial estate. After the driver had his dinner he climbed into his truck cabin and went to bed.

Stefanie and Alberto left for other accommodation and Julio and I had the luxury of sleeping in our cars in the car park in front of the truck stop café with the stone crusher directly in front of us.

I was so tired I could have slept anywhere I had now been on the road for three days and three nights with out a decent wash, or shave, not to mention a change of clothes, so the smell was getting to me.

The next morning Julio and I had a good breakfast and a bit of a wash in the toilets of the café and at 10 am Stefanie and Alberto arrived. We acknowledged each other and the driver of the low-loader appeared and started his engine and slowly drove off the car park into the direction of Tarragona city.

Two hours later we had arrived at our final destination in an industrial zone called Rio Clar Polygon. We had to wait another three hours before the stone crusher was loaded off of the back of low-loader and parked up at the back of a huge warehouse as big as an airplane hanger. The driver of the low-loader was angry for having to wait for so long and was getting angry telephone calls from his boss as he had another job to in Valencia so as soon as the crusher was unloaded, he and his low-loader and flashing lights left.

This industrial estate was to be our home for the next 5 to 6 weeks, guarding the stone crusher day and night with orders that if the stone crusher was to move, then we had to follow it and under no circumstances to leave it.

Static surveillance 24/7

This has got to be one of the most tiring and boring jobs in private investigation and just when you are ready to pack up and go — it all starts happening.

The weather was cold wet and windy for most of the very long days and lonely cold nights on the industrial estate. Tarragona, proved to be taxing and very challenging and I certainly will not forget the six weeks for a long time to come. We had the advantage of a reasonable hotel, where I hired a room that I took turns with all the other agents in sleeping for a couple of hours, getting cleaned up and using the Internet to up-date Mark in the USA.

Back on the industrial estate, every time a low-loader drove on to the estate, the adrenalin started pumping as we thought here we go — the bad guys have come to collect our stone crusher. On average we saw at least 4 low-loaders drive through the estate a day, all well capable of transporting our stone crusher.

We photographed the stone crusher machine morning, noon and night, with the time and date on the photos so that we could prove the existence of the machine. The industrial estate was a dangerous place to be in during the day, as people raced all kinds commercial and private vehicles at break neck speed; as if they were on the Nuremburg Ring. We witnessed at least seven traffic accidents with broken glass all over the road (that no one cleaned up) but this did not slow any of the madmen down.

At night groups of wild dogs were prowling around that had been abandoned and left to fight for survival amongst the rubbish bins.

The shadows of the night were creepy enough and in the distance I could hear the police car sirens screaming into the night. Security guards drove around now and again trying to look as if they were like really busy doing there job but they never once challenged me as to what the hell I was doing there.

I was asked a few times by the local police what I was doing parked up all day and I explained that I was a private investigator and showed the cops my warrant badge and off they went.

One night I witnessed how a group of Arabian looking characters actually tried to break into the yard where our machine was parked; climbing over the wall, they walked right into the alarms systems, so now we had the alarm sirens blaring away. I sent one of my men to call over the security guards that were patrolling the estate but they showed no interest. We could have easily have the crooks cornered but they never touched our stone crusher, so we had no reason to challenge them. By the time the security eventually had come to the place where we had seen the robbers, they were already long gone.

Early that same morning I had seen three young boys that were obviously of Moroccan origin and I would say the oldest could have been 14 years old and the others about 12 years old, playing with a 9 mm hand gun! I could clearly see that this was not a toy gun but what could I say or do — sad but better not to interfere — if you called the police, they would probably take no notice and the young fellah's would have legged it long before anybody arrived or they could even take a pot shot at you.

I was surprised by the amount of foreigners in Tarragona city and suburbs; it seemed that there were more black and Arabian people than Spanish. I had noticed the definite increase in the black Islam, Arab and Moroccan population in Cartagena but here it was so much more.

The yard where our big yellow stone crusher was parked closed at 9 pm and opened at 8am every day.

We were all aware that it would only take 5 minutes to load the stone crusher onto the back of a low-loader and another 5 minutes to drive off the estate, so that gave us a ten minute response time.

I received a telephone call from the 'bad guys' asking to meet with me to discuss a deal that would benefit us all!

I spoke with my client Mark to get his approval to meet them At the same time our lawyers in Granada confirmed that they would receive the Court order to repossess the stone crusher within the next day or two, which would mean that everything would soon be over and that we would take our machine and go home — that sounded too good to be true (and it was).

I met the bad guys at 7 pm in a hotel in the city centre of Tarragona city. Stefanie was on time but her male companion was nearly two hours late, so the meeting did not get started until 9 pm.

Stefanie had told me that this Alberto was the main salesman for selling the machines from her brother Jochen. The deal was: lets stop paying money to lawyers and the Spanish courts and lets start making money again.

Their master plan was:

1. Mark, my client, would have to agree that if we got bad guy number one "Jochen" — Stefanie's brother — out of jail in the States, and dropped all criminal charges against him in three other federal States, then the bad guys would release the stone crusher machine to us and tell us where the other machines are located

that they stole and had in the meantime sold on. They would also sign over to our client 320,000 Euros worth of debt that our client could collect; the reason that bad guys would be so generous was explained to me that once bad guy number one Jochen had been released from jail in the USA, then he would pay back every one from the money he had stashed away from his illegal business.

2. I of course recorded this conversation and also took covert photographs of the meeting and had absolutely no intention of agreeing to their demands.

I said that I would draw up a contract of pre-agreement along the lines that we had talked about at our meeting and that nothing would happen until this had been received and signed in front of a Notary Public. This they agreed to do but of course they never did — there is no honour amongst crooks.

The meeting ended at 10 pm and it was raining again. After the meeting, I left the hotel and got soaked trying to get back to my car. I telephoned Mark and reported everything back to my client and his response was "tell these sons of bitches if they do not give us back my fucking machine I will press criminal charges against all of them bastards and then they can visit each other in jail.

I prepared a pre-agreement contract and sent it to my office to be forwarded on to Mark in the USA and if he agreed to send it after we had translated it on to the bad guys so the ball was now in their court.

I received a telephone call from our legal eagles in Granada informing me that the court in Granada had now made a court ruling (order), impounding the stone crusher machine and placing possession of it under the responsibility of our lawyers meaning basically we are back to square one again, with a year of wasted time and a fortune in costs for both sides.

I started to arrange the organisation and planning of the stone crusher collection thinking that nothing more would or could go wrong.

I had a machine expert, Tom Hyland, flown in from Southern Ireland to drive the stone crusher and to carry out an inspection of the machine. This machine is really a specialised piece of equipment and one mistake can cause a lot of expensive damage.

The next morning being Wednesday, I collected Tom from Reus airport and brought him to our hotel. He was well aware of the whole situation and ready to go.

On Wednesday evening the legal team arrived at the industrial estate in a big Citoen V6 saloon hire car: barrister Alejandro, criminal lawyer Pedro and a Notary. They flew from Granada to Madrid, then Madrid to Barcelona and then hired the car to drive down to meet me I showed them where the stone crusher was parked. Tom was with me waiting for the signal to come in we waited and waited. After half an hour the legal team came out of the yard with the yard owner. Jose and asked Tom to come in and to look at the machine. Tom climbed around the machine in the dark doing the best he could. I was then shocked to hear that the lawyers did not have a court ruling with them as they had said they had, only a paper making our lawyer Alex the depository of the machine and there was no mention of the machine being collected or taken away as we had planned.

After another 30 minutes we left and the yard closed down for the night and we returned to our hotel. The lawyers wanted to go for dinner with the Notary and we felt a bit out of place, so we agreed to meet up in the morning at 9 am sharp and if the yard owner would not hand over the machine, our lawyers would hold him personally responsible for any damage done to the machine and he would also have to pay all sorts of costs. But that was just letting off hot air as nothing happened and the machine was not released and is in fact still in Tarragona.

The next morning the lawyers did not turn up at the agreed meeting time of 9 am, although they were staying in the same hotel as us. They decided to go alone back to the yard and it was very quickly agreed that the machine would not be moved until the

Granada courts had made their final decision.

Tom flew back to Ireland and I drove back home to sort out the paper work and pay all the bills.

I expect there will be more to come on this case but for now its home time after nearly one and half months of ruffling it, being cold, wet and with out any decent food, just waiting for some thing to happen and the lawyers did not even have the correct documents with them!

Figure 5 *arrival of the low loader and stone crusher in Tarragona from Granada after 3 days traveling at 25 MPH and terrible weather.*

Figure 6 *The stone crusher being driven off the back of the low loader in Tarragona where it now stays until its next adventure.*

Figure 7 *The low loader and stone crusher in transit at a truck stop cafe.*

34

Private Investigation and Further Education

Of course the best method of education in any field of work is being on the road and doing it, gathering personal experience that is never mentioned in any university or learning courses; but you also have to update your skills and acquire more knowledge.

I had read all my private investigator study manuals and my long distance learning courses and I had joined English and Spanish trade associations. Slowly things were going in the right direction.

The trade associations normally hold their AGM (Annual General Meeting) in the form of a congress with workshops and seminars to update members on what is what in the PI industry. The most important thing about these meetings is the networking, putting a face to names given during telephone conversations and getting to know new contacts.

At the end of a congress the Grand Gala Banquette is held, a truly special evening to remember. Everyone dresses up as if we are all going to receive an Oscar award. There is a lot of back slapping that goes on and speeches given. Awards are given to the worthy among us for being the best of this and that. Although I have never received an award and I would not know why I should, I have had the honour of giving short speeches at the gala dinners that normally ended up with a bit of a laugh, and actually presenting awards.

Figure 8 *European Congress in Madrid: (L-R) Ray Ashton, Angelina Freyes, the author, Julio Iglasis and Inga*

Figure 9 *(l) Alain Bernier — President du Conseil Europeen des Detectives, (m) Julio Iglesias — President of the Spanish Private Detective Asiciation, (r) Rick Howatson — Central European representative for WAPI*

Figure 10 *The author presenting an award to the President of the Spanish Association of Detectives*

On one such occasion I officially handed an award to the President of the Spanish Detective Association making him an honorary member of the World Association of Professional Investigators; as I walked on to the podium cameras were flashing and there was live TV broadcasting. I do not think that all the media interest was for me but more for the Spanish Minister of Justice, the Attorney General of Spain and the Chief of Police and of course, the President of the Spanish Detective Association.

I had to pinch myself to see if I was dreaming as I had only been a private investigator a couple of years and here I was talking to all those on the top of the tree — the crème de la crème.

After I held my speech I received a lot of applause and a standing ovation. Later I was told that I was the first Englishman ever to speak and hand over an award at a Spanish congress.

At one congress in Zurich, Switzerland after a short speech where I addressed the congress about the European licensing issues, I was so nervous that I needed to have a smoke so I went out to the foyer in the break and two other gentlemen walked out with me, all very smart in our dinner jackets.

One of the gentlemen to my left was a brigadier general from Israel and the gentleman to my right was a brigadier from India.

The Israeli smoked a pipe and the Indian smoked a big cigar, with me in the middle smoking a filter tipped Benson, and getting a headache. I looked at the Israeli brigadier and said that I felt a bit inferior standing between such two distinguished officers, as I had only been a lance corporal in the army.

The Israeli brigadier looked at me and said, "Rick, there is nothing to feel inferior about; Adolf Hitler was only a lance corporal as well."

Figure 11 *The author Rick Howatson and his partner Inga*

Figure 12 *Toni Immossi, the author, Richard Jaques*

35

A Property Search Finds Family

I was in my office one day when I decided to carry out a property search on myself in Spain out of curiosity to see if it would be easy to locate me, as I did not want any bad guys wanting revenge and using me for target practice. You can never be too careful.

The property search was positive and to my complete surprise, my brother's name came up! I found out that he had bought a small house in Spain ten years before, in an area called Campasol, in the next region to me. The nearest town to Campasol is Mazzaron.

With the details I had, I drove to the town hall in Mazzaron, about an hour and half away from where I live. I had only the building details of the property so I had to visit the planning department to get a street name and a house number. This is the sort of job that I would get as a private investigator — here I was doing it for myself!

After a couple of hours searching the maps and plans of four huge estates named sector A, B, C and, that had been built by Spanish construction company MASA, I finally found an address for my brother in sector A. After some door to door enquiries I finally established that my brother lived in sector D — which still did not have a street name or house number after ten years. A friendly neighbour who knew my brother kindly took me to where his house was.

I had not seen my brother since I had been placed in a children's home when I weas ten years old,— he was in Korea in the British

Army at the time. I saw him again briefly for a few hours when I was 25 years old; he was living in England and I was living in Germany. We did not exchange addresses I think because we were all to busy with our own lives at the time.

We had no further contact, not because we did not want to, but because we were always on the move. My brother worked in Saudi Arabia in the banking business and I was diving around the world. Who would have ever guessed that all these years later we would be next county neighbours living in the same country!

I rang his door bell and my brother opened the door but didn't recognise me. "Who are you?," he asked.

"I am your younger brother," I replied. Shock was in his eyes. There was no hugging at first, just a cold hand shake and a "do come in."

That was two years ago. Unfortunately my brother's wife Dorothy had passed away 6 months before, after having been paralysed for ten years following a stroke. The reason my brother stopped travelling and came to Spain was for the better quality of life for his wife, with whom he had been married for 52 years. I was amazed at the loving way that my brother John took care of his wife and he really did a magnificent job of it too. I am so proud my brother is such a wonderful man.

Since my sister in-law's passing, my brother and I have become very close and after 45 years of not knowing each other, we now speak several times every day.

Figure 13 *John and Rick Howatson*

Explanation of Terms

1 — **Zombie Walk** — an organised public gathering of people who dress up in zombie costumes. Usually taking place in an urban centre, the participants make their way around the city streets and through shopping malls in a somewhat orderly fashion and often limping their way towards a local cemetery or other public space; or a series of taverns in the case of a zombie pub crawl. (Courtesy of Wikipedia)

2 — **Guardia Civil** — In Spain there are three police forces: the National Police, the Local Police and the Guardia Civil.

Spanish National Police

The Spanish National Police was formed in 1824 and they are considered to be equivalent to any other European police force with the same powers and of course they are armed.

Figure 14 Police car used by the National Police in Spain.

Figure 15 Police car used by the
National Police in Spain.

Spanish Local police

The Spanish Local police are employed by the local town halls in Spain and are used for crowd management and traffic cops in the cities. They are also armed.

Guardia Civil

The Civil Guard was founded in 1844 during the reign of Queen Isabel II of Spain by the Basque Navarrese aristocrat Francisco Javier Girón y Ezpeleta, second Duke of Ahumada. The policing done by the Civil Guard was carried out earlier by the Holy Hermandad. The first academy of "guardias civiles" was established in the town of Valdemoro, south of Madrid, in 1855.

The Guardia Civil's first job was to restore and maintain security in the Spanish countryside. The end of the First Carlist War had left the Spanish landscape scarred by the destruction of civil war, and the government moved fast to prevent the increasing danger of banditry in rural areas. Based on the model of light infantry used by Napoleon in his European campaigns, the Guardia Civil was born as a police force with high mobility that could be deployed irrespective of inhospitable conditions and that was able to patrol large areas of the countryside. Its members, called 'guardias', maintain to this date a basic patrol unit formed by two agents, usually called a "pareja" (a pair), in which one of the 'guardias' will initiate the intervention while the second 'guardia' serves as a backup to the first one.

The Modern Force

Today the Guardia Civil is a police force in a developed democratic society subject to the checks and supervision expected in a democratic society. The guardias' proven effectiveness throughout history in controlling banditry and in addressing the subsequent challenges and tasks given them, meant that additional tasks have been added regularly to their job description. Today, they are primarily

Figure 16 Police on horseback.

responsible for policing and/or safety regarding the following (but not limited to) areas and/or safety related issues (given in no special order): highway patrol, drugs and anti-smuggling operations, customs and ports of entry control, safety of prisons and safeguarding of prisoners, weapons licenses and arms control, security of border areas, bomb squad and explosives, security in rural areas and in locations with less than 10,000 inhabitants, anti-terrorism; coast guard, police deployments abroad (embassies); intelligence and counter-intelligence gathering, cyber- and internet crime, hunting permits and environmental law enforcement..

Peacekeepers

The Civil Guard has won international respect for their work as peacekeepers in United Nations sponsored operations, including operations in Bosnia and Herzegovina, Angola, Congo, Nicaragua, Haiti, East Timor and El Salvador. They served with the Spanish contingent in the war in Iraq, mainly in intelligence gathering, and they lost seven 'números'. The Guardia Civil is also known as el instituto armado ("the armed institution") and la benemérita ("the good-deserving"). They served with great distinction in the Spanish colonies, including Cuba, Puerto Rico, the Philippines and Morocco.

The Guardia Civil has a sister force in Costa Rica also called the Guardia Civil. The Costa Rican 'guardias' often train at the same academy as regular Spanish officers. Characteristics

They typically patrol in pairs. Their traditional hat is the tricornio, originally a tricorne. Its use now is reserved to parades or ceremonies, being now substituted by a cap, a beret or the characteristic "gorra teresiana".

Members of the Guardia Civil often live in garrisons (casa-cuartel) with their families. Family members of guardia civiles have fallen victim to attacks initially addressed against the police force.

Since the Guardia Civil must accommodate the families of its "guardias", it was the first police force in Europe that accommodated a same-sex partner in a military installation.

The symbol of the Guardia Civil consists of the Royal Crown of Spain, a sword and a fasces. The different units have variations of this symbol. (Courtesy of Wikipedia)

3 — **Baguette** — a variety of bread distinguishable by its much greater length than width, and noted for its very crispy crust. The standard size of a baguette is approx. 5 or 6 cm, but can be up to a metre in length. It is also known in English as a *French stick* or a *French loaf.* (Courtesy of Wikipedia)

Figure 17 *My good friends from the Guardia Civil*

Tips For Starting A New Business In Europe

Anyone contemplating going into business should put together a complete business plan and also get good advice. If you don't know how, do some research on the Internet regarding business plans for service agencies? When planning, be honest with the figures, otherwise you will only shoot yourself in the foot. This should be done *before* going into business. If you haven't done this, you need to sit down *now* and start working on it. (I didn't even have an Internet connection for my little laptop at the time but I was still working on it, preparing my plan.) Every business needs a marketing plan — take the time to sit down and work one out — and promotion: advertising, direct contact, email or newsletters. So how does a covert undercover private investigator go about it?

One way is advertising in the yellow pages and trade magazines — get quotations first — but your most important tool in your new business enterprise is: *contacts*. Everyone is a contact; renew old friendships, make new ones because the very best method of promoting your business is by word of mouth. A good website selling your services is also crucial, as more people start to look for information this way.

Once you start, you should have in place a method to determine the results of any marketing. Without this, you can waste a lot of money and lose business that you should have gotten.

If you are just breaking even or maybe even adding to your over draft each month, you need to re-examine what you are doing very carefully. It may be time to either raise your prices or get out of the business. If you are not making a profit over and above your basic expenses — business and home, you need to make some serious decisions. Or you will enter the circle of death, where one day all your bills creep up from behind and gobble you up! It would seem as if you never existed and nobody gives a toss if you make it or not. The world only likes lovers and winners.

No one can tell you what you should charge for your services — only you will know that answer. And, yes, local competition does have input in your decision but I say if you want reliable quality then you have to pay for it.

(Just remember, the competition never sleeps.)

21472309R00132

Printed in Great Britain
by Amazon